To the visitor, the tourist, Sicily was Taormina, Catania, Syracuse—golden beaches, laughing peasants.

But there was another, darker place in the hinterland. A savage landscape, sterile, barren, where the struggle was not so much for a living, but for survival. A world where the key-word was *omerta*, which you could call manliness for want of a better translation. Manliness, honor, solve your own problem, never seek official help, all of which led to the concept of personal vendetta and was the breeding ground for Mafia.

This was the world where I grew up.

This was the world of my grandfather.

And this was the world which now threatened to destroy me.

In the Hour
before Midnight

by

Jack Higgins

FAWCETT GOLD MEDAL • NEW YORK

IN THE HOUR BEFORE MIDNIGHT

Published by Fawcett Gold Medal Books, a unit of CBS Publications, the Consumer Publishing Division of CBS Inc.

THIS BOOK CONTAINS THE COMPLETE TEXT OF THE ORIGINAL HARDCOVER EDITION PUBLISHED BY DOUBLEDAY and COMPANY, INC.

ISBN: 0-449-13954-9

Printed in the United States of America

6 7 8 9 10

For Ken and Janet Swinhoe—
and the other Amy

In the Hour before Midnight

1

I SUPPOSE he must have died during the night, but I only became aware of it in the heat of the day.

Not that it made much difference, not even the stench of putrefaction. In that place everything died except me, Stacey Wyatt, the great survivor. There had been times when I would have greeted death as a friend, cooperated with him actively, but that was long ago—too long. Now, I waited in a limbo of my own devising, proof against all they could do to me.

I'd been in the Hole for three days now, which was what it was called by prisoner and guard alike—a place of darkness and furnace heat where you rotted in your own filth and died from lack of air.

It was the fourth time I'd been put down since they'd brought me to the labour camp at Fuad, each dose coinciding with one of Major Husseini's inspections. In the June war he had been one of the thousands whipped in Sinai and left to stumble home through one of the worst deserts on earth. He had seen his command crumble, men die around him by the hundred from thirst and the sun had burned its way into his brain, starting a fire that

9

could never be put out, leaving him with a hatred for Israel which had developed into a kind of paranoia.

He seemed to see Jews everywhere, a constant threat to Egypt's safety. As I was an enemy of his country, tried and convicted by law of subversive activities, I too must be a Jew who had somehow managed to conceal the fact from the court.

The previous July, I'd brought a forty-foot launch in from Crete with gold bullion for a gentleman from Cairo who was supposed to meet me on a beach at Ras el Kana-yis, part of a complicated exchange process by which someone, somewhere, finally made a fortune. I never did find out exactly what went wrong, but a couple of UAR gunboats appeared rather inconveniently, plus a half company of infantry on the beach. The economy benefited to the extent of half a ton of gold and John Smith, this year's unknown American citizen, went down for seven years.

After six months in a city goal, they transferred me to Fuad, a fishing village ninety miles from Alex. There were about thirty of us there, mostly political offenders condemned to work on the roads in chain gangs, although in this case, we were building a new pier. We were guarded by half-a-dozen peasant conscripts and a civilian overseer called Tufik, a large, fat man who sweated a lot and smiled all the time. He had two wives and eight children and treated us with remarkable gentleness under the circumstances, although I think he was due a bonus if we finished by the end of July, which meant that he needed all the labor he could get and didn't want anyone to die on him.

The man who had gone to a happier place during the night had been a special case, a Bedu from the south who had repeatedly tried to escape, a fierce, proud animal who had never slept under a roof in his life. For him, any kind of prison had been an automatic death-sentence and everyone had known that, even Tufik. But there was general camp discipline to consider and he'd gone into the Hole to encourage the others. He'd already been there a week when I joined him.

I was wearing a kind of wooden halter padlocked around the neck, my wrists chained to it at shoulder level. It was impossible to lie down or even to stand, for if I tried within those narrow confines, the ends of the halter caught against the rough walls, jarring my neck painfully. So I sat there in the heat, floating in my own dark limbo, reading my favourite books page-by-page, an excellent mental exercise, or when that palled, returning to the next phase of a monumental and highly personal course of self-analysis. I had started with childhood, the earliest memories—Wyatt's Landing ten miles from Cape Cod and my father's family who had never liked me although I hadn't realised that fact until his death in Korea in nineteen fifty-three when I was ten. It was only afterwards that it was made plain that the Wyatt blood in me was tainted, for my mother was Sicilian. So to Sicily we went, to the great cool villa on the cliffs above the sea outside Palermo, to my grandfather, Vito Barbaccia to whom men touched their hats, who ordered the police from here to there like chessmen, who scowled and made the politicians tremble.

Vito Barbaccia, *capo mafia*, Lord of Life and Death . . .

I was working my way through my freshman year at Harvard when there was a sudden banging above my head, a chain rattled, and from the scraping, I knew that the stones were being pulled away. When the wooden trap was lifted, the sunlight flooded in, momentarily blinding me. I closed my eyes, blinked and looked through a soft, golden haze that told me it was late afternoon.

Major Husseini crouched at the edge, small and wizened, dried up by the Sinai sun that had deranged him, his olive face pitted from the smallpox. A couple of soldiers stood beside him and Tufik was there looking distinctly unhappy.

"So, Jew," Husseini said in English for although my Arabic had understandably improved over the past ten months, he considered it an insult to use the language of his fathers with someone like me.

He stood up and laughed contemptuously. "Look at him." He gestured to the others. "Squatting in his own excrement like an animal." He looked down at me again. "Do you like that, Jew? You like to sit there smeared with your own dung?"

"It's not so bad, Major," I told him in Arabic. "A monk once asked Bodidharma, what is Buddha? The master replied, dried dung."

He stared down at me in a kind of bewilderment, so perplexed that he momentarily lapsed into Arabic himself. "What are you talking about?"

"You'd need brains to make sense of it."

The trouble was that as I'd used Arabic, they all understood. The skin tightened across his cheeks and the eyes contracted. He turned to Tufik.

"Have him up. Hang him in the sun for a while. I'll deal with him when I get back."

"Something to look forward to," I said and for some reason started to laugh weakly.

There wasn't much to Fuad; forty or fifty small flat-roofed houses around a wide square, a crumbling mosque, no more than a couple of hundred inhabitants. It was miserably poor like most of these Egyptian villages although the new pier was supposed to change all that. The sea was about four hundred yards away, the blue Mediterranean. Nice to be beside if you were on the beach at Antibes. I got a quick glimpse of it before they removed my halter and strung me by the wrists from a kind of wooden gallows in the centre of the square.

It was supposed to be painful and would have been under normal circumstances, but I had been through so much during those past months that pain in itself meant very little to me any longer. In the heat of the day it could have been unpleasant, but not now in the late afternoon. In any case I had discovered from past experience, that by focussing on some object in the middle distance, a kind of self-hypnosis could be induced that made two or three hours seem considerably less.

Beside the guard post, a United Arab Republic flag drooped from a white-painted flagstaff and beyond, three men and a boy were driving a flock of several hundred sheep in from the desert. The thick cloud of dust raised by their hooves was blown towards the village like spreading smoke and the flag lifted momentarily.

It was all very Biblical, very Old Testament except that one of the shepherds carried an automatic rifle, which proved something although I wasn't sure what. God, but I was dry. I closed my eyes and breathed deeply for a while. When I opened them again nothing had changed. The same square, the same squalid little houses, the same uncanny lack of people. They had sense and were staying indoors while Husseini was around.

Tufik emerged from his office with a canteen of water and crossed towards me, sweat springing from every pore. It was an effort for him to scramble up on to the old packing case that the two guards had stood on when stringing me up, but he made it and forced the neck of the canteen between my teeth. He gave me a short swallow and poured the rest over my head.

"You will be reasonable, Mr. Smith, when he returns. Promise me that. It will only be worse for you if you annoy him further."

He stared at me anxiously, mopping his face with a soiled handkerchief. I was intrigued. For one thing, he'd called me mister, certainly the first time that had happened and he was worried about me—too worried. It didn't really make sense, but Husseini arrived before I could take it further.

His Land-Rover scattered the sheep a hundred yards on the other side of the village and braked to a halt outside the guard post. Husseini got out and came towards me. He stood perhaps ten yards away, staring up at me, his eyes full of hate, then turned abruptly and went into the guard post.

The sheep arrived, flooding in between the houses, spilling across the square as they pushed towards the pool on the far side. The boy I had noticed earlier was perhaps ten or eleven, small and dark and full of energy, running up and down whistling and flapping his arms in the air to keep them on the move. His three companions were typical Bedu in shabby robes, each man with his burnoose folded across his face as a protection against the heavy dust raised by the sheep.

They passed by, heads down, pushing the flock hard, minding their own business, bells clanking in the stillness. It was very quiet, the sun half-way below the horizon now. Another thirty minutes and the gang would be returning from the pier and their day's work.

The sheep were at the water, fighting each other for the best positions and the shepherds squatted against a wall watching them. The door of the guard post opened and Husseini emerged and came towards me, the two soldiers at his heels. When they cut me down, I collapsed in a heap on the ground. He said something or other, I couldn't quite catch what it was, and they picked me up between them and followed him across the square to Tufik's place.

The fat man lived alone except for some old woman who came in each day to cook and wash for him and the house he had commandeered doubled as an office. There was a roll-top desk, two wooden chairs and a table.

Husseini barked an order and the two soldiers sat me on one of the chairs and bound my arms firmly.

It was then that I noticed his whip, real rhino from the look of it, guaranteed to take the flesh from a man's spine. He took off his tunic and started to roll up his sleeves very carefully. Tufik looked frightened to death and sweated more than ever. The two soldiers stood against the wall and Husseini picked up the whip.

"Now, Jew," he said, bending it like a bow in his two hands. "To start with, a dozen. After that we shall see."

"Major Husseini," a voice said softly in English.

Husseini turned sharply and I lifted my head. Beyond him in the doorway stood one of the shepherds. His right hand went to his burnoose, pulling it away, revealing a tanned, wedge-shaped face and the kind of mouth that looked as if it might twist into a smile at any moment, but seldom did, grey eyes, cold as water over stone.

"Sean?" I croaked. "Sean Burke? Could that be you?"

"As ever was, Stacey."

His left hand came out of his robe holding a Browning automatic. His first shot took Husseini in the shoulder twisting him round so that I looked into his face as he died. The second blew away the back of his head, driving him past me and into the wall.

The two soldiers stared stupidly, eyes widening in horror, their rifles still slung from their shoulders, and died that way as a machine pistol smashed through the window and cut them down in two long bursts.

There was a kind of silence and Tufik was the first to speak, the words falling over themselves to get out. "I was worried, terribly worried. I though you weren't coming, that something might have gone wrong."

Burke ignored him. He came forward slowly and leaned over me. "Stacey?" he said and touched my cheek gently with his left hand. "Stacey?"

There was pain on his face, something I had never seen

before, and then that terrible killing rage for which he was so notorious. He turned on Tufik.

"What have you done to him?"

Tufik's eyes widened. "What have I done, Effendi? But I am the one who has made all this possible."

"I've just decided I don't like your prices."

The Browning swept up, Tufik cried out in fear and cowered in the corner. I shook my head and said weakly, "Leave him alone, Sean, he could have been worse. Just get me out of here."

There was a momentary hesitation and then the Browning disappeared inside the robe. Tufik slid down on to his knees and started to cry weakly.

I might have known who the other two would be. Piet Jaeger the South African, one of the few survivors of our old company in the Katanga campaign, and Legrande, the ex-O.A.S. man Burke had recruited in Stanleyville when we had re-formed. Jaeger was driving Husseini's Land-Rover and Legrande helped Burke lift me into the back seat. Nobody said very much and there was obviously some kind of time-table in operation.

Fuad was still quiet as the grave when he drove out along the so-called coast road, passing the column of prisoners marching in from their day's work on the way.

"You haven't got long," I whispered.

Burke nodded. "We're dead on time. Don't worry."

A mile farther on, Jaeger swung off the road and took us through sand dunes to the edge of a broad flat beach. As he switched off the motor another sound filled the air, and a plane came in off the sea no more than two or three hundred feet above the surface of the water. Legrande produced a Very pistol and fired a flare and the plane turned sharply and dropped in for a perfect landing.

It was a Cessna, I recognised that much as it taxied towards us, but there was no time to stand around. They hustled me forward as the cabin door swung open and pushed me inside. The others followed and as Legrande fastened the door, the Cessna was already turning into the wind, her engine note deepening.

Burke held a flask to my mouth and I choked as brandy burned its way into my stomach. When the coughing had subsided, I smiled weakly. "Where to now, Colonel?"

"First stop Crete," he said. "We'll be there in an hour. Good thing, too. You could do with a bath."

I took the flask from him and swallowed again and leaned back in my seat as a warm and wonderful glow spread throughout my body. Life began again, that was all I could think of. As the Cessna lifted into the air and turned out to sea, the sun died behind the horizon and night fell.

2

I FIRST met Sean Burke in Lourenco Marques in Portuguese Mozambique in the early part of 1962 in a waterfront cafe called the Lights of Lisbon. I was playing piano at the time, one of the more useful by-products of an expensive education, but wholly for money.

For reasons which aren't important at the moment, I was an aimless drifter at the grand old age of nineteen, working my way from Cairo to the Cape in easy stages. I was in Lourenco Marques because I'd only had enough money to take me that far on boarding the coastal steamer at Mombasa, which didn't worry me particularly. I was young and fit, running so hard from the past that my only concern was to discover what lay beyond each day's horizon.

In any case, I liked Lourenco Marques. It had a kind of baroque charm and in those days at least, a complete absence of the kind of racial tensions I'd noticed elsewhere in Africa.

The man who ran the Lights of Lisbon was named Coimbra, a thin, cadaverous Portuguese with one interest in life—money. He had a hand in most things as far as I could judge and didn't have a scruple in the world. Whatever you wanted, Coimbra could get it for you at a price. We boasted the finest selection of girls on the coast.

I noticed Burke the moment he came in, although his enormous physique would have made him stand out anywhere. I think that was the thing which struck one most about him—the air of sheer physical competence and controlled power that made men move out of his way, even in a place like that.

He was dressed for the bush in felt hat, shooting jacket, khaki pants and sand boots. One of the girls made a pass at him, a quadroon with a skin like honey and the kind of body that would have had a bishop on his knees. Burke looked through her, not over her, as if she simply didn't exist and ordered a drink.

The girl was called Lola and as we'd been more than good friends, I felt like telling him he was missing out on a damn good thing, but maybe that was just the whisky talking. In those days I wasn't too used to it and it was dangerously cheap. When I looked up, he was standing watching, a glass of beer in one hand.

"You want to lay off that stuff," he said as I poured another. "It won't do you any good, not in this climate."

"My funeral."

I suppose that was the right kind of reply for the tough, footloose adventurer I fondly imagined myself to be at that time and I toasted him. He challenged me calmly, his face quite expressionless and when I raised the glass to my lips, it took a real physical effort. The whisky tasted foul. I gagged and put the glass down hurriedly, a hand to my mouth.

His expression didn't change. "The barman tells me you're English."

Which was what I thought he was at the time for his Irish upbringing was indicated more by tricks of speech and phrasing than accent.

I shook my head. "American."

"You don't sound like it."

"I spent what they term the formative years in Europe."

He nodded. "I don't suppose you can play 'The Lark in the Clear Air'?"

"As ever was," I said and moved into a reasonably straight rendering of the beautiful old Irish folk song.

It lacked John McCormack, but wasn't bad though I do say it myself. He nodded soberly when I finished. "You're good—too good for this place."

"Thanks," I said. "Is it all right if I smoke?"

"I'll tell the barman to send you a beer," he replied gravely.

He returned to the bar and a moment later one of Coimbra's flunkeys tapped him on the shoulder. There was a short conversation and they went upstairs together.

Lola came across, yawning hugely. "You're losing your touch," I told her.

"The Englishman?" She shrugged. "I've met his kind before. Half a man. Big in everything except what counts."

She moved on and I sat there thinking about what she had said, working my way through a slow blues. At that time I was inclined to think she was talking into the wind, probably out of a kind of professional pique at being snubbed. A man didn't have to be homosexual just because he wasn't particularly attracted to women although I've never seen any virtue in not indulging at every opportunity in what is one of life's greatest pleasures as far as I'm concerned. The Sicilian half of me discovered women early.

I came to the end of the number I was playing and lit a cigarette. For some reason there was one of those sudden lulls that you sometimes get with a crowd anywhere. Everyone seemed to stop talking and the whole thing became curiously dreamlike. It was as if I was outside looking into the packed room and things moved in a kind of slow motion.

What was I doing here on the rim of the dark continent, Africa all around me? Faces everywhere, looming through the smoke, black, white, brown and subtle variations in between, riff-raff, not even a common humanity holding us together, all running from something.

Suddenly I'd had enough. In a way, I'd taken a look, not so much at myself as I was then, but at what I would soon become and I didn't like what I'd seen. I was hot and sticky, sweat trickling from my armpits, and I decided to change my shirt. I realise now, of course, that I was only looking for some excuse to go upstairs.

My own room was on the third floor, Coimbra's apartment on the second, the girls being down below. As a rule it was quiet up there because that was the way Coimbra like it, but now, as I paused at the end of the passage, I was aware again of that same strange stillness I had experienced earlier.

The voices, when I heard them, seemed far away and I walked on, aware that someone was speaking angrily. The first door opened into a kind of anteroom. I went in cautiously and moved through darkness to where a thousand fingers of light pierced a lattice screen.

Coimbra was seated at his desk, one of his heavies, Gilberto, at his back holding a gun. Herrara, the man who had brought Burke up from the cafe, leaned against the door, arms folded.

Burke was standing a couple of yards away from the desk, legs slightly apart, hands in the pockets of his bush jacket. I could see him in profile and his face might have been carved from stone.

"You don't seem to understand," Coimbra was saying. "No one was interested in your proposition, it's as simple as that."

"And my five thousand dollars?"

Coimbra looked as if he was fast losing his patience. "I have been put to considerable expense in this matter—considerable expense."

"I'm sure you have."

"Now you are being sensible, Major, in business these things happen. One must be prepared to take risks for quick returns. And now you must excuse me. My men will escort you. This is a rough district. It would desolate me if anything were to happen to you."

"I'm sure it would," Burke said dryly.

Gilberto smiled for the first time and hefted the Luger in his hand and Burke took off his bush hat, wiping his face with the back of his right hand, looking suddenly beaten.

But I could see what they could not. Inside the crown of his hat an old short-barrelled Banker's special was held in place by a spring clip. He shot Gilberto from cover, so to speak, slamming him back against the wall, turned and covered Herrara, who was starting to draw.

"I don't think so," Burke said and I was aware of the power in the man, the vital force.

He made Herrara face the wall and searched him quickly. And Coimbra, man of surprises to the end, opened a silver cigar box and produced a small automatic.

I had a friend once who took up golf and was a scratch man within three months. He had a natural flair for the game just as some people have language kinks and others can rival computers in mental calculation.

On one memorable Sunday afternoon during my first month at Harvard, another student took me to a local pistol club. I'd never fired a gun in my life, yet when he put a Colt Woodsman in my hand and told me what to do, I experienced a new feeling. The gun became a part of me and the things I did with it in one short hour had astonished everyone there.

So I was a natural shot with something of a genius for

hand guns, but I had never aimed at a human being. What happened next seemed so natural that in retrospect it was frightening. I flung open the door, dropped to one knee and grabbed for Gilberto's Luger where it lay on the floor. In the same moment, I shot Coimbra through the hand.

Burke swung, crouched for action, a tiger ready to spring, his own gun in one hand, Herrara's in the other. Although I didn't realise it then, it said a lot for his control that he didn't shoot me as a reflex action.

He gave me one brief glance and I thought he would smile. Instead, he opened the outside door, listened, then closed it again.

"The kind of place where people mind their own business," I told him.

He walked slowly to the desk. Gilberto crouched against the wall clutching his chest, blood at the corner of his mouth. His eyes were open, but he was obviously in deep shock. Coimbra had gone very pale and held his right hand under his left arm as if trying to stop the bleeding. Burke touched him between the eyes with the barrel of his revolver.

"Five thousand dollars."

Even then, Coimbra hesitated and I put in quickly, "There's a safe inside the walnut cabinet by the door."

Burke thumbed back the hammer of his revolver with an audible click and Coimbra said hastily, "The key is in the cigar box under the tray."

"Get it," Burke told me. "Bring whatever you find."

There was certainly considerably more than five thousand dollars in the cash box I brought to the desk although I never did find out exactly how much. Burke took the lot, the neat packets of banknotes vanishing into the capacious pockets of his bush jacket.

"One must be prepared to take risks for quick returns, isn't that what you said, Coimbra?"

But Coimbra was past caring and fainted across the

desk. Herrara still leaned against the wall, hands flat. Burke turned and hit him almost casually, striking with clenched fist at the base of the skull. Herrara went down with a groan.

The Banker's special was returned to its clip inside the crown of the bush hat and he replaced it on his head, adjusting the angle of the brim in the mirror. He turned to face me.

"First rule in the bush," he said. "Walk, don't run. Remember that on the way out."

We left by the side entrance which was usually kept open for those clients who wanted direct access to the girls and didn't welcome publicity. A Ford truck was parked just around the corner from the cafe, an African dozing behind the wheel. Burke told me to get in the back, spoke to the driver and joined me.

As the truck started to move, I said, "Where to now?"

"The old army airstrip at Caruba. Do you know it?"

"I've only been in town a couple of weeks. That job at the Lights of Lisbon wasn't intended to be my life's work. I was just trying to raise the price of a ticket to Cape Town."

"Any special reason?"

"A man has to have an aim in life."

He accepted it, looking quite serious and nodded. "That was good shooting back there. Where did you learn?"

When I explained he was obviously surprised. At that time I didn't realize how good I must have looked because it wasn't until later that I learned that I had acted instinctively like a real professional who always aims for the shooting hand with his first bullet, knowing that a dying man can still get off a shot at him.

We moved out through the edge of town. There were no longer any street lamps and we were shrouded in darkness. After a while he asked if I had my passport.

I reached for my wallet instinctively and nodded. "About all I have got."

And then, as if it had only just occurred to him, he said, "My name is Burke, by the way—Sean Burke."

"Stacey Wyatt." I hesitated. "Didn't I hear Coimbra call you Major?"

"That's right. I was twenty years in the British Army— Paratroops. Left last year. I've just been granted a commission by the Katanga government."

"The Congo?" I said.

"I'm forming a special unit to help keep order. Coimbra was supposed to find me a few men. The bastard didn't even try. Now I've got an old DC3 waiting at the airstrip and no one to fly out in her."

"Except me."

The words were out without thought and impossible to go back on, even if I'd wanted to. There was pride for one thing, but there was more to it than that. For some reason I found that I wanted his approval. I don't suppose a psychologist would have had much difficulty in analysing the situation. I'd lost my father too early in life for a growing boy plus the whole of that side of my family. Now I was running hard, trying to erase the memory of the events of the last few terrible months that had taken my mother and had left me with only one individual on top of earth who really cared for me—my grandfather. The one person I was afraid to love.

Burke's voice cut in on my thoughts. "You mean it?" he said softly.

"Coimbra was the first person I ever shot at in my life," I told him. "I think I should make that clear in fairness to you."

"Four hundred thousand francs a month," he said, "and everything included."

"Including a shroud? I hear it's rough up there."

He changed—altered completely, became almost a different person. He laughed out of the darkness, reached over and squeezed my arm. "I'll teach you, Stacey—everything you need to know. We'll cut a path from one end of the Congo to the other and come out laughing with our pockets full of gold."

Thunder rumbled beyond the horizon like distant drums and rain started to fall, heavy nd warm, thumping against the canvas roof. The air was electric. I was seized with excitement. I suppose the simple fact was that I wanted to be like him. Tough, unafraid, not caring, able to look the world straight in the eye and stare it down.

God, but I was happy then—happy for the first time in years as the truck lurched through the night, filling my nostrils with the dust of Africa.

3

BURKE'S BASTARDS, that was the name some newspaperman came up with after that first foray into Katanga. We lost a lot of men, but others lost more and the newspaper stories certainly helped recruiting. They built Burke up into something of a legend for a while and then forgot him, but by then our reputation as an elite corps was secure. There was no more difficulty in finding men and Burke was able to pick and choose.

And they were marvellous days—the best I had ever known. Hard living, hard training. I felt my strength then for the first time, tried my courage and found, as I suspect most men do, that I could keep going when afraid, which, when you come down to it, is all that really matters.

Burke was never satisfied. During one lull between engagements, he even forced us through paratroop training, dropping over Lumba Airport from an old De Havilland Rapide. A month later we used it for real and parachuted into a mission station in the Kasai just ahead of a force of simbas, the savage guerrillas native to the area. We pushed our way out through a couple of hundred miles of unfriendly bush bringing eight nuns with us.

They made Burke a colonel for that little jaunt and I got a captain's commission around the time I would have been in my third year at Harvard. Life was good then, full of action and passion as it should be, and the money poured in as he had promised it would. Two years later, those of us who were left were lucky to get out in what we stood up in.

Contrary to popular opinion, most mercenaries in the Congo were there for the same reason that young men used to join the Foreign Legion. It was what happened when you experienced the reality that was the trouble. I had seen what was left of settlers who had been quartered on the buzz saw of a lumber mill. I had also known mercenaries who had been in the habit of disposing of prisoners by locking them inside old ammunition boxes and dropping them into Lake Kivu, but only when they were too tired to use them for target practise.

In between the two extremes, I had changed, but Piet Jaeger hadn't altered in the slightest. He came from the sort of bush town in the northern Transvaal where they still believed kaffirs didn't have souls and was one of the few survivors of the original commando.

Strangely enough, when one considered his background, Piet was no racist. He had joined us because the chance of a little action and some money in his pocket contrasted favourably with the family farm and the kind of father who carried a Bible in one hand and a *sjambok* in the other, which he was as likely to use on Piet as the kaffirs who were unfortunate enough to work for him. He had stayed because he worshipped Burke, had followed him gladly to hell and back and would again without a qualm.

I watched him now in the mirror as he removed my beard with infinite care, a bronzed young god with close-cropped fair hair, a casting director's dream for the part of the young SS officer torn by conscience who sacrifices himself for the girl in the final scene.

Legrande leaned in the doorway, his amiable peasant face expressionless, a Gauloise dropping beneath the heavy moustache. As I said, most of those who went to the Congo were in search of adventure, but there were exceptions and Legrande was one of them, a killer who destroyed without mercy. An OAS gunman, he'd come to the Congo for sanctuary and in spite of my youth had always shown me a kind of grudging respect. I suspect for my skill at arms as much as anything else.

Very carefully Piet removed the hot towel and stood back and a stranger stared out at me from the mirror, bones showing in the gaunt, sun-blackened face, dark eyes looking through and beyond, still and quiet, waiting for something to happen.

"Flesh on your bones, that's all you need," Piet said. "Good food and lots of red wine."

"And a woman," Legrande said with complete seriousness. "A good woman who knows what she's about. Balance in all things."

"Plenty of those in Sicily so they tell me," Piet said.

I glanced up at him sharply, but before I could ask him what he meant, one appeared from the terrace and hesitated, uncertainty on her face as she looked at us. She was obviously Greek and perhaps thirty or thirty-five. It's hard to tell with peasant women at that age. She had masses of night-black hair that flowed to her shoulders, an olive skin, the lines just beginning to show, and kind eyes.

Legrande and Piet started to laugh and Piet gave the Frenchman a shove towards the door. "We'll leave you to it, Stacey."

Their laughter still echoed faintly after the door had closed and the woman came forward, and put two clean towels and a white shirt on the bed. She smiled and said something in Greek. It isn't one of my languages so I tried Italian, remembering they'd been here during the war.

That didn't work and neither did German.

I shrugged helplessly and she smiled again and for some reason ruffled my hair as if I were a schoolboy. I was still sitting in front of the dressing table where Piet had shaved me and she was standing very close, her breasts on a level with my face. She wore no perfume, but the dress she had on, a cheap cotton thing, had just been laundered and smelled fresh and clean and womanly, filling me with the kind of ache I had forgotten existed.

I watched her cross the room and go out through the window and took a few very deep breaths. It had been a long time, a hell of a long time, and Legrande, as always, had put his finger right on the spot. I took off my robe and started to dress.

The villa was sited on a hillside a couple of hundred feet above a white sand beach. It was obviously a converted farmhouse and someone had spent a small fortune making it just right.

I sat at a table on the edge of the terrace in the hot sun and the woman appeared with grapefruit and scrambled eggs and bacon on a tray with a very English pot of tea. My favourite breakfast. Burke, of course—he thought of everything. I don't think I've ever tasted anything quite like that meal sitting there on the edge of the terrace looking out over the Aegean to the Cyclades drifting north into the haze.

There was a curious air of unreality to it all and things carried the knife-edge sharpness of the wrong kind of dream. Where was I? Here or in the Hole?

I closed my eyes briefly, opened them again and found Burke watching me gravely.

He wore a faded bush shirt and khaki slacks, an old felt hat leaving his face in shadow, and carried a .22 Martini carbine.

"Keeping your hand in?" I asked.

He nodded. "I've been shooting at anything that moves. It's that kind of morning. How do you feel?"

"Considerably improved. That doctor you provided pumped me full of one good thing after another. Thanks for the breakfast, by the way. You remembered."

"I've known you long enough, haven't I?" He smiled, that rare smile of his that almost seemed to melt whatever it was that had frozen up inside, but never quite succeeded.

Seeing him standing there in the felt hat and bush shirt I was reminded again of that first meeting in Mozambique. He was just the same. Magnificently fit with the physique of a heavyweight wrestler and the energy of a man half his age and yet there were changes—slight, perhaps, but there to be seen.

For one thing, the eyes were pouching slightly and there was an edge of flesh to the bones that hadn't been there before. If it had been anyone else I'd have said they'd been drinking, but liquor was something he'd never shown any interest in—or women, if it came to that. He'd always barely tolerated my own need for both.

It was when he sat down and removed his sunglasses that I received my greatest shock. The eyes, those fine grey eyes, were empty, clouded with a kind of opaque skin of indifference. For a brief moment when anger had blazed out of them back at Fuad in the labour camp, I had seen the old Sean Burke. Now I seemed to be looking at a man who had become a stranger to himself.

He poured a cup of tea, produced a pack of cigarettes and lit one, something I'd never seen him do before and the hand that held it trembled very, very slightly.

"I've taken up a vice or two since you last saw me, Stacey boy," he said.

"So it would seem."

"Was it bad back there?"

"Not at first. The prison in Cairo was no worse than

you'd expect anywhere. It was the labour camp that wasn't so good. I don't think Husseini had been right in his head since Sinai. He thought there was a Jew under every bed."

He looked puzzled and I explained. He nodded soberly when I finished. "I've seen men go that way before."

There was silence for a while as if he couldn't think of anything to say and I poured another cup of tea and helped myself to one of his cigarettes. The smoke bit into the back of my throat like acid and I choked.

He started to rise, immediately concerned. "What is it? What's wrong?"

I managed to catch my breath and held up the cigarette. "Something I had to manage without back there. It tastes like the first one I ever had. Don't worry—I'll persevere."

"But why start again?"

I inhaled for the second time. It tasted rather better and I grinned. "I agree with Voltaire. There are some pleasures it's well worth shortening life for."

He frowned and tossed his own cigarette over the balustrade as if attempting to right some kind of balance, for what I had said went completely against his own expressed beliefs. For him, a man—a real man—was completely self-sufficient, a disciplined creature controlling his environment, subject to no vices, no obsessive needs.

He sat there now, a slight frown still in place, staring moodily into space, and I watched him closely. Sean Burke, the finest, most complete man-at-arms I had ever known. The eternal soldier, an Achilles without a heel on the surface, and yet there were depths there. As I have said, he seldom smiled, for some dark happening had touched him in the past, lived with him still. His spiritual home was still the army, the real army, I was certain of that. By all the rules he should have had a staggeringly successful career in it.

During his brief moment of fame in the Congo, the newspapers had unearthed his past in detail. Born in Eire, son of an Anglo-Irish Protestant minister who had fought passionately for the Republic in his day, Burke had joined the Irish Guards at seventeen during the Second World War and had soon transferred to the Parachute Regiment. He'd earned a quick M.C. as a young lieutenant at Arnhem and, as a captain in Malaya during the emergency, a D.S.O. and promotion to major. Why then had he resigned? There was no official explanation that made any kind of sense. Burke himself had said at the time that the army had simply got too tame. And yet there had been a story in one paper, cautiously told and full of innuendo, that hinted at another explanation—the possibility of a courtmartial, had he not resigned, that would have sent him from the army utterly disgraced—and I remembered again our first meeting at the Lights of Lisbon. What was it Lola had said of him? Half a man. *Big in everything except what counts.* It was possible. All things were possible in this worst of all possible worlds.

But that was not true, that my real self simply couldn't accept on a morning like this. It was a beautiful world, this world outside the Hole, a place of warmth and air and light, sweet sounds, sun and colour to dazzle the mind.

He stood up and leaned on the balustrade, looking out over the sea. "Quite a place, isn't it?"

I nodded. "Who owns it?"

"A man called Hoffer—Karl Hoffer."

"And who might he be when he's at home?"

"An Austrian financier."

"Can't say I've heard of him."

"You wouldn't. He isn't too keen on newspaper publicity."

"Is he rich?"

"A millionaire and that's by my standards, not your Yankee one. As a matter of fact that was his gold you were running the night the Egyptians jumped you."

Which was an interesting piece of information. Millionaire financiers who indulged in a little gold smuggling on the side were about as rare within my experience as the greater blue-tailed goose. Herr Hoffer sounded like a man of infinite possibilities.

"Where is he now?"

"Palermo," Burke said and there was a kind of eagerness in his voice as if, by asking, I'd made things easier for him.

Which explained Piet's remark about the girls in Sicily.

"When you got me into the plane I asked you where we were going," I said. "You told me Crete first stop. Presumably Sicily is the second?"

"A hundred thousand dollars split four ways plus expenses, Stacey." He sat down again and leaned across the table, fingers interlocking so tightly when he clasped his hands that the knuckles showed white. "How does that sound to you?"

"For a contract?" I said. "A contract in Sicily?"

He nodded. "A week's work at the most and easily earned with you along."

The whole thing was beginning to fall neatly into place. "By me, you mean Stacey the Sicilian, I presume?"

"Sure, I do." Whenever he got excited the Irish side of him floated to the top like cream on milk. "With your Sicilian background we can't go wrong. Without you, I honestly think we wouldn't stand a chance."

"That's very interesting," I said, "but tell me something, Sean. Where would I have been sitting right this minute if this Sicilian business hadn't come up? If you hadn't needed me?"

He stared at me, caught at one fixed point in time like a butterfly pinned to a collector's board, tried to speak and failed.

"You bastard," I said. "You can stick your hundred thousand dollars where Grandma had the pain."

His hands came apart, fists clenched, the skin of his

face turned milk-white with the speed of a chemical reaction and something stirred in the depths of those grey
eyes.

"We've come a long way since the Lights of Lisbon,
haven't we, Colonel?" I got up without waiting for a reply
and left him there.

In the cool shadows of my bedroom, anger possessed
me like a living thing and my hands were shaking. There
was sweat on my face and I opened the top drawer in the
dressing table to search for a handkerchief. Instead I
found something else. A pistol—the kind of side-arm I
had always carried, a replica of the one the Egyptians had
relieved me of on that dark night a thousand years ago—a
Smith & Wesson .38 Special with a two-inch barrel in an
open-sided spring holster.

I fastened the holster to my belt slightly forward of the
right hip, pulled on a cream-coloured linen jacket I found
behind the door and slipped a box of cartridges into one
of the pockets.

I found a pack of cards on a table in the living room as
I knew I would where Legrande and Piet were around,
and went out, taking a path down the hillside to the white
beach below. One way of releasing tension is as good as
another and in any event it was obviously time to see if
I'd forgotten anything.

4

IN face-to-face combat, any soldier in his right mind would rather have a good rifle in his hands than a pistol any day of the week. In spite of what they say in the Westerns, a normal handgun isn't much use beyond fifty yards and most people would miss a barn door at ten paces.

Having said that, there's no doubt that with someone who knows what he's about, there's nothing to equal a good handgun for close quarters work.

I used to favour a Browning P35 automatic, which is standard issue in the British Army these days, mainly because it gave me thirteen shots without having to reload, but automatics have certain snags to them, lots of bits and pieces that can go wrong, and no professional gunman I've ever met would use one from choice.

In an ambush at Kimpala, I had a simba bearing down on me like an express train, a three-foot panga ready in his right hand. I shot him once, then the pin fell on a dud round. It doesn't happen all that often and in a revolver the cylinder would have kept on turning, but this was an automatic. The Browning jammed tight and my friend, doped up to the eyeballs, kept right on coming.

We spent an interesting couple of minutes on the ground and the memory stayed with me for some time afterwards. From then on I was strictly a revolver man. Only five rounds if you leave one chamber empty for safety, but completely dependable.

When I got down to the beach, it was calm and still, the sea like a blue-green mirror, the sun so strong that the rocks were too hot to touch and light bounced back from the white sand, dazzling the eye and objects blurred, became indistinct.

I took off my jacket and loaded the Smith & Wesson carefully with five rounds, then hefted it first in my left hand, then in my right. Already the old alchemy was beginning to work. Heat burned its way through the thin soles of my shoes, scoured my back, became a part of me as this gun was a part, the butt fitting easily to my hand. Nothing special about it, no custom-built grip or shaved trigger. A first-rate, factory-made, deadly weapon, just like Stacey Wyatt.

I took out the pack of cards, lined five of them up in a thin crack on the edge of a lump of basalt and marked out fifteen paces. There had been a time when I could draw and hit a playing card five times at that distance inside half a second, but a lot had happened in between. I dropped into a crouch, drew and fired, arm extended, gun chest-high. The echoes died flatly away across the oily sea. I reloaded at once and went forward.

Two hits out of five. Even if the other three rounds hadn't been too far off target it still wasn't good enough. I returned to the firing line, adopted the conventional target stance, gun at eye level, and fired at each card in turn, taking my time.

I got all five as I had expected, put up fresh cards and

tried again. I still stayed with the target stance, but this time emptied the gun fairly rapidly.

Once more a hit on each card. I was ready to go back to square one again. I put up more cards, turned and found Burke at the bottom of the path. He stood there watching, anonymous in his dark glasses, and I turned on the firing line, drew and fired, and five shots so close together that they sounded like one continous roll. As I reloaded, he went forward and got the card. Four hits—three close together, one at twelve o'clock. A whisker higher and it would have missed altogether.

"A little time, Stacey," he said. "That's all you need."

He held out his hand and I gave him the Smith & Wesson. He tried the balance for a moment, then pivoted and fired using his own rather peculiar stance, right foot so far forward that his left knee almost touched the ground, gun straight out in front of him.

He had five hits, three close together, the other two straying towards the right-hand edge. I showed him the card without comment. He nodded gravely, no visible satisfaction on his face.

"Not bad. Not bad at all. A tendency to kick to the right a little. Maybe you could lighten the trigger."

"All right, you've made your point." I started to reload. "Why didn't you bring the heavy brigade with you?"

"Piet and Legrande?" He shook his head. "This is between you and me, Stacey—no one else."

"A special relationship, is that what you're trying to say? Just like America and England."

He didn't exactly boil over, but there was anger there, pulsating just beneath the surface of things.

"All right, so I got you out a little later than I'd intended. Have you any idea how much organising it took? What it cost?"

He stood there, waiting, I think, for some gesture from

me and, when it didn't come, turned abruptly and walked to the water's edge. He picked up a stone, pitched it away from him half-heartedly, then slumped down on a rock and sat there gazing into the distance looking strangely dejected. For the first time since I'd known him he seemed his age.

I holstered the Smith & Wesson and squatted beside him. I offered him a cigarette without a word and he refused with a small and peculiarly characteristic gesture of one hand as if brushing something away from him.

"What happened, Sean?" I said. "You're different."

He removed the sunglasses, ran a hand over his face and smiled faintly, looking out to sea. "When I was your age, Stacey, the future held a kind of infinite promise. Now I'm forty-eight and it's all somewhere behind me."

It sounded like the sort of remark he'd spent a lot of careful work on beforehand, a characteristic of the Irish that didn't just start with Oscar Wilde.

"I get it," I said, "this is dust and ashes morning."

He carried straight on as if I hadn't said a word. "Life has a habit of catching up on all of us sooner or later, I suppose. You wake up one morning and suddenly, for the first time ever, you want to know what it's all about. When you're on the margin of things like me, it's probably too late anyway."

"It's always too late to ask that kind of question," I said, "from the day you're born."

I was aware of a certain irritation. I didn't want this sort of conversation and yet here I was in mid-stream in spite of the faint suspicion I'd had for a while now where Burke was concerned, that somehow I was being conned, caught in a spider's web of Irish humbug served up by a talent that wouldn't have disgraced the Abbey Theatre.

He glanced at me and there was urgency in his voice when he said, "What about you, Stacey? What do you believe in? Really believe in with all your guts?"

I didn't even have to think any more, not after the Hole. "I shared a cell in Cairo with an old man called Malik."

"What was he in for?"

"Some kind of political thing. I never did find out. They took him away in the end. He was a Buddhist—a Zen Buddhist. Knew by heart every word Bodhidharma ever said. It kept us going for three months."

"You mean he converted you?" There was a frown on his face. I suppose he must have thought I was going to tell him I couldn't indulge in violence any more.

I shook my head. "Let's say he helped shape my philosophy. Me, I'm a doubter. I don't believe in anything or anybody. Once you believe in something you immediately invite someone else to disagree. From then on you're in trouble."

I don't think he'd heard a word I'd been saying or perhaps he just didn't understand. "It's a point of view."

"Which gets us precisely nowhere." I flicked what was left of my cigarette into the water. "Just how bad are things?"

"About as rough as they could be."

Not only the villa belonged to Herr Hoffer. It seemed the Cessna was also his and he'd provided the cash that had gone into the operation that had got me out of Fuad.

"Do you own anything besides the clothes you stand up in?" I asked.

"That's all we came out of the Congo with," he pointed out, "or do I need to remind you?"

"There have been several bits of banditry in between, as I recall."

He sighed and said with obvious reluctance, "I might as well tell you. We were in for a percentage of that gold you were caught with at Ras el Kanayis."

"How big a percentage?"

"Everything we had. We could have made five times its value overnight. It looked like a good proposition."

"Nice of you to tell me."

I wasn't angry. It didn't seem to be all that important any more and I was interested in the next move.

"No more wars, Sean?" I asked. "What about the Biafrans? Couldn't they use a good commando?"

"They couldn't pay in washers. In any case, I've had enough of that kind of game—we all have."

"So Sicily is the only chance?"

It was obviously the moment he'd been waiting for—the first real opening I had given him.

"The last chance, Stacey—the last and only chance. One hundred thousand dollars plus expenses . . ."

I held up my hand. "No sales talk. Just tell me about it."

God, but I'd come a long, long way in those six years since Mozambique. Little Stacey Wyatt telling Sean Burke what to do and he took it, that was the amazing thing.

"It's simple enough," he said. "Hoffer's a widower with a stepdaughter called Joanna—Joanna Truscott."

"American?"

"No, English and very upper-crust from what I hear. Her father was a baronet or something like that. She's an honourable anyway, not that it means much these days. Hoffer's had trouble with her for years. One scrape after another. Sleeping around—that kind of thing."

"How old is she?"

"Twenty."

The Honourable Joanna Truscott sounded promising. "She must be quite a girl."

"I wouldn't know—we've never met. Hoffer has business interests in Sicily. Something to do with the oilfields at a place called Gela. You know it?"

"It was a Greek colony. Aeschylus died there. They say he was brained by a tortoise shell dropped by a passing eagle." He gazed at me blankly and I grinned. "I had an expensive education, Sean, remember? But never mind. What about the Truscott girl?"

"She disappeared about a month ago. Hoffer didn't notify the police because he thought she was off on some binge or other. Then he got a ransom note from a bandit called Serafino Lentini."

"An old Sicilian custom. How much?"

"Oh, it was modest enough. Twenty-five thousand dollars."

"Did he go to the police?"

Burke shook his head. "Apparently he's spent enough time in Sicily to know that doesn't do much good."

"Wise man. So he paid up?"

"That's about the size of it. Unfortunately this Serafino took the money, then told him he'd decided to hang on to her for a while. He also indicated that if there was any trouble—any sign of the law being brought in—he'd send her back in pieces."

"A Sicilian to the backbone," I said. "Does Hoffer have any idea where he's hanging out?"

"The general area of a mountain called Cammarata. Do you know it?"

I laughed. "The last place God made. A wilderness of sterile valleys and jagged peaks. There are caves up there that used to hide Roman slaves two thousand years ago. Believe me, if this Serafino of yours is a mountain man the police could chase him for a year up there without even seeing him and helicopters don't do too well in that kind of country. The heat of the day does funny things to the air temperature. Too many down drafts."

"As bad as that?"

"Worse than you could ever imagine. The greatest bandit of them all, Giuliano, operated in the same kind of territory and they couldn't catch him, even when they brought in a couple of army divisions."

He nodded slowly. "Could we do it, Stacey? You and me and the heavy brigade?"

I thought about it. About the Cammarata and the heat and the lava rock and about Serafino who might already have handed the girl on to the rest of his men. When I replied, it wasn't because the thought made me sick or angry or anything like that. From the sound of her, the Honourable Joanna might well be having the time of her life. I don't honestly think I was even thinking of my end of the money. It was more than that—something deeper—something personal between Burke and me which I couldn't have explained at the moment even to myself.

"Yes, I think it could be done. With me along it's just possible."

"Then you'll come?"

He leaned forward eagerly, a hand on my shoulder, but I wasn't going to be caught that easily.

"I'll think about it."

He didn't smile, showed no emotion of any kind, and yet tension oozed out of him like dirty water and in a second he was transformed into the man I'd always known.

"Good lad. I'll see you later then. Back at the villa."

I watched him climb the path and disappear. For the moment I'd had enough shooting. The sea looked inviting and I moved a little farther along the beach, stripped and went in.

At that point the cliffs merged into hillside sparsely covered with grass and wild flowers grew in profusion. I climbed half-way up and lay on my back, the sun warm on my naked flesh, staring through narrowed eyelids at a white cloud no bigger than my hand, allowing my whole body to relax, making my mind a blank, another trick hard-won from those months in prison.

The world was a blue bowl and I floated in it, drowsing in the scented grass and slept.

Waking was a return to a heavy stillness. I was aware of flowers, the grass at eye-level like a jungle, the woman watching me from a few yards away. Was it an accidental encounter, or had she been sent by Burke? I wasn't angry, but strangely calculating considering the circumstances. I watched her through slitted eyes, apparently still asleep, making no move. She stayed perhaps two or three minutes, her face quite expressionless, then went away carefully.

When she had gone, I sat up, dressed and went down to the beach again feeling rather excited. In a way, the whole thing had become a kind of game with Burke making a new move as I countered the old one.

The cards were where I had left them together with my box of ammunition and, when I moved to the firing line, I had never known such power, such certainty. I drew, fired and was reloading within the second, my old self again, the Stacey from before the Hole . . . and yet not the same.

This time I fired left-handed, drawing on the cross from my waistband, and knew before I checked what I would find.

Five hits . . . five hits on each card tightly grouped. I tore them into very small pieces, scattered them into the sea and went back up to the villa.

I slept during the afternoon, waking just before night fell, and yet I lay there without moving when Burke entered the room to check on me and softly departed.

When it was quite dark I got up, pulled on a pair of pants and ventured onto the terrace. I could hear voices near at hand, followed the sound and paused at the window of what was obviously his bedroom. He was sitting at a desk in one corner and Piet was standing beside him, his fair hair golden in the lamplight.

Burke glanced up at him and smiled—a new kind of

smile, one I'd never seen before—patted his arm and said something. Piet went out like some faithful hound about his master's business.

Burke opened a drawer, produced what looked suspiciously like a bottle of whisky, uncorked it and swallowed, which for a man who didn't drink was quite a trick. He put the bottle back in the drawer when the door opened and the woman entered.

I got ready to leave, mainly because whatever else I am I'm no voyeur, but there was no need. He simply sat there looking very much the colonel and talked, presumably in Greek, which I knew he spoke well after a couple of years in Cyprus during the Emergency.

I eased back into the shadows as she left and moved back to my room. The whole thing was certainly packed full of human interest and drama and I lit a cigarette, lay on the bed and thought about it all.

The story—that was the really weak link. The story about the Honourable Joanna and the rampant Serafino. Oh, it was possible, but strangely incomplete like a Bach fugue with page three missing.

Somewhere thunder rumbled menacingly. The Gods were angry perhaps? *Oh, mighty Zeus forgive us.* The old Greek tag drifted up from some dusty schoolroom to haunt me along with wine-dark seas, Achilles and his heel and cunning Odysseus.

I didn't hear her come in, but when lightning crackled out to sea, it picked her from the night standing just inside the french window. I made no sound. When it flared again, she had come closer, the dress on the floor behind her, her body a thing of light and mystery, dark hair brushing the full breasts.

In the darkness following, her hands were on me, her mouth, her flesh against mine. In one single savage movement I had her by the hair, my hand tightening cruelly.

"What did he tell you to do?" I demanded. "Anything I wanted, anything to keep me happy?"

Her body ached in pain and yet she did not struggle and when the lightning flickered again, highlighting the heavy breasts, I saw that her eyes were turned towards me and there was no fear there.

My fingers slackened in her hair and she subsided. I gently patted her face, her lips turned into the palm of my hand. So, it had come to this? Stacey the satyr—fill one half of his bed for him and keep him happy. The rest was easy. Just like my English breakfast—Burke thought of everything. Only the piano was missing and he'd probably tried hard enough to get hold of one.

I went to the french window and stood looking out at the flickering sky. Suddenly, and for no accountable reason, the whole thing struck me as really being very funny —a monstrous game for children with motive laid bare to such a degree that it was ridiculous.

Burke wanted me—needed me. In exchange I got twenty-five thousand dollars and all my more carnal needs supplied. Now what well-bred satyr could complain at that?

I nodded slowly. Right. Let it be so. I would play his game through as I had done before, but this time perhaps a rule or two of my own might be in order.

Behind me was the softest of movements and I sensed her presence there in the darkness. I reached out and pulled her close. She was still naked and shivered slightly. I could smell the mimosa, heavy and clinging on the damp air. The whole electric world waited for a sign. It came and the heavens opened, rain falling straight from sky to earth.

The freshness filled my nostrils, drowning the womanly scent of her. I left her there, moved out on the terrace and stood, face turned up to the rain, mouth half-open, laughing as I hadn't laughed in a long, long time, ready to take on the world again and beat it at its own dark game.

5

IT WAS Holy Week when we arrived in Palermo, something which I'd completely forgotten about. We drove in the thirty-five kilometres from the aerodrome at Punta Raisi and the black Mercedes saloon which had met us bogged down in the crowded streets. It finally came to a halt in deference to a religious procession which wound its way through the crowds, an ornate Madonna rising on a catafalque high above our heads.

During the whole of the run from Crete, Burke had been moody and irritable and now he lowered the window and looked out with ill-concealed impatience.

"What's all this?"

"A procession of the mysteries," I told him. "This kind of thing goes on during Holy Week all over Sicily. Everything else grinds to a halt. They're a very religious people."

"It doesn't seem to have rubbed off much on you," he commented sourly.

Piet Jaeger glanced at me anxiously. How much he knew of what had been said between Burke and myself, of the hardness of the bargaining, I wasn't sure, but the change in our relationship had been plain enough during the past three days.

"Oh, I don't know," I said. "Didn't you notice the Virgin had a knife through her heart? That's Sicily for you —the cult of Death everywhere. I'd have thought I fitted in rather nicely."

He smiled reluctantly. "You could be right at that."

I turned to Piet. "Oh, you'll love it. It's one hell of a place. On All Saints' Day the children are given presents from the dead. The graves are probably the best kept in the world."

Piet grinned, obviously relieved, but Legrande who was sitting beside the driver was hot and tired, his eyes tinged with yellow which didn't look too good. Maybe one of the several fevers he'd picked up in that Viet prison camp after Dien Bien Phu was about to plague him.

"What is this, a conducted tour?" he demanded.

I ignored him and leaned out of the window as the Mercedes pushed its way through the crowd. The girls were a little more fashionably dressed than when I had last been here and so were the younger men, but I could smell incense and candle grease, hear voices chanting beyond the square. The crowd parted and the penitents appeared looking remarkably like the local chapter of the Ku Klux Klan in pointed hoods and long white robes.

No, nothing had changed—not down there beneath the surface where it counted.

About seven miles out of Palermo on the coast road to Messina you come to the beaches of Romagnolo, a favourite spot for city-dwellers at weekends. Hoffer's villa was a couple of miles farther on. It didn't look more than a year or two old and had obviously been specially designed to fit into the hillside site, rising above us on three different levels with what looked like a Moorish garden crowning the highest roof.

The whole was surrounded by a high wall and we had to wait to be identified at the gates by a guard who carried an automatic rifle slung from one shoulder.

"Why the private army?" I asked Burke.

"Hoffer's a rich man. Since this business with the girl he's been getting worried. Maybe they'll have a go at him next."

Which seemed reasonable enough. Kidnapping was, after all, one of Sicily's oldest industries and in any case I'd been to parties at houses in Bel Air where the gate-keeper was armed. Sicily wasn't the only society where the rich got neurotic about the prospect of someone trying to take it away from them.

On the other hand, Hoffer certainly seemed to cover all his bets. Even our driver, a burly Norman-Sicilian with ginger hair, was wearing a shoulder holster, a fact which his tight-fitting chauffeur's uniform made rather too obvious.

There was a scent of wisteria in the air and I could see the purple blooms in profusion on the other side of the drive. It was all very lush, very Mediterranean with palm trees carefully placed to make every vista please and yet its very harmony was vaguely unsettling. Things were a little too perfect, a design on paper, product of some expert mind, planned to produce results in the shortest possible time. An instant garden.

The Mercedes braked in a gravelled circle in front of the entrance and a couple of houseboys came down in a hurry to get the bags. As they went back up the steps a woman appeared on the porch and looked down at us languidly.

She was small, dark-haired and with the kind of body that can only be described as ripe. She was Sicilian to the backbone, twenty-two or -three by my judgment, although she looked older as southern women often do. She was wearing black leather riding pants, a white silk shirt knotted at her waist and a Cordoban hat.

"And who might that be?" Piet demanded.

"Hoffer's girl friend. I'll see what the situation is."

Burke went up the steps and they held a brief, whispered conversation that died as I joined them.

"Hoffer isn't here at the moment," Burke told me. "Had to go to Gela on business last night, but he's due back later on this afternoon. I'd like you to meet Signorina Rosa Solazzo. Rosa, my good friend Stacey Wyatt."

Her English was excellent. She held my hand briefly, but didn't remove her sunglasses. "A pleasure, Mr. Wyatt. I've heard a great deal about you."

Which might have been true or could have been merely conventional politeness. Hoffer didn't sound like the sort who needed any confidante and from the look of her it seemed more likely that he kept her around solely to help him through those long night watches.

She turned to Burke. "Rooms are arranged for you. The servants will take you up. I suppose you'd like to shower and change so I'll order the meal for an hour from now."

She left and we followed the houseboys through a large cool hall where everything seemed to swim in green and gold and up a short flight of stairs to the second tier of the building.

Piet and Legrande shared, but Burke and I were honoured with separate rooms. Mine was long and narrow, one wall consisting of sliding glass doors opening to a balcony overlooking the garden. The furniture was English and in excellent taste, the carpet so thick that it deadened all sound, and when I tried the other door I found my own bathroom.

The houseboy put my bag on the bed and left and I went and turned on the shower. When I came back into the bedroom, Burke was standing by the window.

He managed a smile. "The rich full life, eh?"

"Something like that. I don't know about you, but I'm going to have a shower."

He was obviously eager to please and moved to the door at once. "A good idea. I'll see you downstairs in an hour."

But I had other plans. I gave myself about a minute and a half under an ice-cold needlespray and changed, pulling on a clean shirt and a lightweight suit in blue tropical worsted. A pair of gold-framed sunglasses completed the outfit.

I hesitated over the Smith & Wesson, but this was Sicily after all. I clipped the holster to my belt on the right hand side, left the room quickly and went downstairs.

There seemed to be no one about and I paused on top of the steps outside the front door. The Mercedes was still there, the driver going over the windscreen with a wash leather.

Rosa Solazzo said from behind, "You are going somewhere, Mr. Wyatt?"

I turned and said cheerfully, "Yes, into Palermo if that's all right with you."

"But of course, I'll tell Ciccio to take you wherever you want."

It was nicely done and without the slightest hint of hesitation. The local dialect in Sicily is similar to the Italian spoken in the rest of Italy except for one or two different vowel sounds and an accent you could cut with a knife. She switched over to it as we went down the steps.

"The American wants to go into Palermo," she told Ciccio. "Take him wherever he wishes and watch him closely."

"You do that, Ciccio," I said as he held open the door for me, "and I'll slice your ears off."

Or at least that was the gist of what I told him in the kind of Sicilian you hear on the Palermo waterfront and nowhere else.

His mouth sagged in surprise and the Solazzo woman's

head snapped round. I ignored her frown, got in the back of the Mercedes. Ciccio slammed the door and slid behind the wheel. He glanced at her inquiringly, she nodded and we moved away.

I made him drop me in the Piazza Pretoria because it seemed as good a place as any and I'd always been fond of that amazing baroque fountain and the beautifully vulgar figures of river nymphs, tritons and lesser gods. At the northern end of the bay, Monte Pellegrino towered in the late afternoon sun and I went on past the beautiful old church of Santa Caterina, turned into the Via Roma and walked towards the central station.

In a side street, I came across a small crowd waiting to go into a marionette theatre. They were mainly tourists— German from the sound of them. They were certainly in for a shock. Even in decline, the old puppet masters refuse to change their ways and the speeches are delivered in the kind of Sicilian dialect, that even a mainland Italian can't follow.

On the way in from the airport, I'd noticed one or two of the old hand-painted carts with brass scroll-work, drawn by feather-tufted horses, but on the whole, most of the farmers seemed to be running around on three-wheeler Vespas and Lambrettas. So much for tradition, but just before I reached the Via Lincoln, I saw a carriage for hire standing at the curbside just ahead of me.

It was past its prime, the woodwork cracking, the leather harness splitting with age, and yet it had been lovingly cared for, the brasswork glinting in the sunlight, and I could smell the wax polish on the upholstery.

The driver looked about eighty years old with a face like a walnut and a long white moustache curling up around each cheek. From the moment I spoke he quite obviously took me for a Sicilian.

In Palermo it is necessary to make a bargain with a

horse cab driver for any journey, however short, which can be rough on the tourist, but I had no trouble—no trouble at all. When I told him where I wanted to go, his eyebrows went up and a look of genuine respect settled on his face, which was hardly surprising. After all, no one visits a cemetery for fun and, to a Sicilian, death is a serious business. Ever-present and always interesting.

Our destination was an old Benedictine monastery about a mile out of town towards Monte Pellegrino and the cab took its time getting there, which suited me perfectly because I wanted to think.

Did I really wish to go through with this? Was it necessary? To that, there could be no answer for, when I considered the matter seriously, I discovered with some surprise that I could do so with a complete lack of any kind of passion, which certainly hadn't been the case at one time. Once, my mind had been like an open wound, each thought a constant and painful probe, but now . . .

The sun had gone down and clouds moved in from the sea, pushed by a cold wind. When we reached the monastery I told him to wait for me and got down.

"Excuse me, signor," he said, "you have someone laid to rest here? Someone close?"

"My mother."

Strange, but it was only then, at that moment, that pain moved inside me, rising like floodwater, threatening to overwhelm me so that I turned and stumbled away as he crossed himself.

A side entrance took me through a large cloister with arcades on each side. In a small courtyard a delightful Arabic fountain sprang into the air like a spray of silver flowers and beyond, through an archway, was the cemetery.

On a fine day the view over the valley to the sea was quite spectacular, but now the lines of cypress trees bowed to the wind and a few cold drops of rain splashed on the stonework. The cemetery was large and very well kept, used mainly by the cream of Palermo's bourgeois society.

I followed the path slowly, gravel crunching beneath my feet, and for some reason everything assumed a dream-like quality. Blank marble faces drifted by as I passed through a forest of ornate ornaments.

I had no difficulty in finding it and it was exactly as I had remembered. A white marble tomb with bronze doors, a life-size statue of Santa Rosalia of Pellegrino on top, the whole surrounded by six-foot iron railings painted black and gold.

I pressed my face against them and read the inscription. *Rosalia Barbaccia Wyatt—mother and daughter—taken cruelly before her time. Vengeance is mine saith the Lord.*

I remembered that other morning when I had stood here with everyone who mattered in Palermo society standing behind me as the priest spoke over the coffin, my grandfather at my side, as cold and as dangerously quiet as those marble statues.

At the right moment, I had turned and walked away through the crowd, broken into a run when he called, had kept on running till that famous meeting at the Lights of Lisbon in Mozambique.

There was a little more rain on the wind now, I could feel it on my face, I took a couple of breaths to steady myself, turned from the railings and found him standing watching me. Marco Gagini, my grandfather's strong right arm, his bullet-proof waistcoat, his rock. I read somewhere once that Wyatt Earp survived Tombstone only because he had Doc Halliday to cover his back. My grandfather had Marco.

He had the face of a good middleweight fighter, which was what he had once been, the look of a confident gladi-ator who has survived the arena. The hair was a little more grizzled, there were a few more lines on the face, but otherwise he looked just the same. He had loved me, this man, taught me to box, to drive, to play poker and win—but he loved my grandfather more.

He stood there now, hands pushed into the pockets of his blue nylon raincoat, watching me, a slight frown on his face.

"How goes it, Marco?" I said easily.

"As always. The *capo* wants to see you."

"How did he know I was back?"

"Someone in Customs or Immigration told him. Does it matter?" He shrugged. "Sooner or later the *capo* gets to know everything."

"So it's still the same, Marco?" I said. "He's still *capo*. I thought Rome was supposed to be clamping down on Mafia these days."

He smiled slightly. "Let's go, Stacey, it's going to rain."

I shook my head. "Not now—later. I'll come tonight when I've had time to think. You tell him that."

It had been obvious to me from the beginning that he had been holding a gun in his right-hand pocket. He started to take it out and found himself staring into the muzzle of the Smith & Wesson. He didn't go white—he wasn't the sort—but something happened to him. There was a kind of disbelief there, at my speed, I suppose, and at the fact that little Stacey had grown up some.

"Slowly, Marco, very slowly."

He produced a Walther P38 and I told him to lay it down carefully and back off. I picked the Walther up and shook my head.

"An automatic isn't much use from the pocket, Marco, I'd have thought you'd have known that. The slide nearly always catches on the lining with your first shot."

He didn't speak, just stood there staring at me as if I were a stranger, and I slipped the Walther into my pocket. "Tonight, Marco, about nine. I'll see him then. Now go."

He hesitated and Sean Burke moved out from behind a

marble tomb five or six yards behind him, a Browning in one hand.

"If I were you I'd do as he says," he told Marco in his own peculiar brand of Italian.

Marco went without a word and Burke turned and looked at me gravely. "An old friend?"

"Something like that. Where did you spring from?"

"Rosa got another car out quick and I followed the Mercedes into town—no trouble. It got interesting when we discovered you had someone else on your tail. Who was he?"

"A friend of my grandfather. He wants to see me."

"He must have one hell of an information service to know you were here so quickly."

"The best."

He moved to the railings and read the inscription. "Your mother?" I nodded. "You never did tell me about it."

And I found out that I wanted to, which was strange. It was as if we were on the old footing again or perhaps I was in that kind of mood where I would have told it to anyone.

"I said my mother was Sicilian, that my grandfather still lived here, but I don't think I ever went into details."

"Not that I recall. I believe you mentioned his name, but I'd forgotten it until I saw it again just now on the inscription there."

I sat on the edge of a tomb and lit a cigarette. I wondered how much I could tell him, how much he could possibly understand. To the visitor, the tourist, Sicily was Taormina, Catania, Syracuse—golden beaches, laughing peasants. But there was another, darker place in the hinterland. A savage landscape, sterile, barren, where the struggle was not so much for a living, but for survival. A world where the keyword was *omerta*, which you could call manliness for want of a better translation. Manliness, honour, solve your own problem, never seek official help, all of which led to the concept of personal *vendetta* and was the breeding ground for Mafia.

"What do you know about Mafia, Sean?"

"Didn't it start as some kind of secret society in the old days?"

"That's right. It came into being in a period of real oppression. In those days it was the only weapon the peasant had, his only means of any kind of justice. Like all similar movements, it grew steadily more corrupt. It ended up by having the peasant, the whole of Sicily by the throat." I dropped my cigarette and rubbed it into the gravel. "And still does in spite of what the authorities in Rome have been able to do."

"But what has this got to do with you?"

"My grandfather, Vito Barbaccia, is *capo mafia* in Palermo, in all Sicily. Number one man. Lord of Life and Death. There are something like three million Sicilians in the States now and Mafia moved over there as well and became one of the main branches of syndicated gangsterism. During the last ten years, quite a few Mafia bosses in the States have been deported. They've come back home with new ideas—prostitution, drugs and so on. An old-fashioned *mafioso* like my grandfather doesn't mind killing people, but he just doesn't go in for that kind of thing."

"There was trouble?"

"You could put it that way. They placed a bomb in his car—a favourite way of getting rid of a rival in those circles. Unfortunately, it was my mother who decided to go for a drive."

"My God." There was shock and genuine pain on his face.

I carried on, "Believe it or not, but I didn't know a damn thing about it, or maybe I didn't want to know. I came home on vacation after my first year at Harvard and it happened on the second day. My grandfather told me the facts of life the same evening."

"Did he ever manage to settle up with the man responsible?"

"Oh, I'm sure he did. In fact, nothing's more certain." I stood up. "I'm beginning to feel rather hungry. Shall we go back?"

"I'm sorry, Stacey," he said. "Damned sorry."

"Why should you be? Ancient history now."

But I believed him for he seemed sincere enough. The wind moaned through the cypress trees, scattering rain across the path, and I turned and walked back towards the monastery.

6

I WENT to bed for a while after we'd eaten. Sleep came easily to me at that time, simply by closing the eyes, and I seldom seemed to dream. When I opened them again it was seven-thirty by the bedside clock and almost dark.

Somewhere I could hear the murmur of voices and I got to my feet, pulled on a bathrobe and padded across to the glass doors that opened on to the terrace.

Burke was standing in the courtyard below, one foot on the rim of the ornamental fountain. His companion was a thick-set man with close-cropped white hair who looked in better shape than he probably was, thanks to a tailor who knew how to cut cloth.

There was nothing ostentatious about him. He'd resisted the impulse to wear more than one ring and displayed only the regulation inch of white cuff as if following someone's instructions to the letter. I think it was the tie which spoiled things—Guards Brigade, which didn't seem likely—and when he produced a platinum case and offered Burke a cigarette, he looked about as real as his garden.

He accepted a light, turned away slightly, running a hand over his hair with a rather feminine gesture, and saw me standing there at the edge of the balcony.

He had obviously cultivated the instant smile. "Hello there," he called. "I'm Karl Hoffer. How are you?"

"Fine," I said. "You provide excellent beds."

His voice was the first surprise. Pure American—no Austrian accent at all as far as I could judge.

He smiled at Burke. "Heh, I like him," then looked up at me again. "We're just going to have a drink. Why don't you join us? Good chance to talk business."

"Five minutes," I said and went back into the bedroom to dress.

As I went down to the hall, Rosa Solazzo appeared from the dining room followed by one of the houseboys carrying a tray of drinks. All the best dresses were English that year. Hers must have set Hoffer back five hundred dollars at least, a cloud of red silk like a flame in the night, setting her hair and eyes off to perfection.

"Please," she said, reached up and straightened my tie. "There, that is better. I felt very foolish this afternoon. I didn't know."

She'd spoken in Italian and I replied in kind. "Didn't know what?"

"Oh, about you. That your mother was Sicilian."

"And who told you that?"

"Colonel Burke."

"Life's just full of surprises, isn't it?" I said. "Shall we join the others?"

"As you wish."

I think she took it as some kind of dismissal, but she certainly didn't seem annoyed, although I suppose a woman in her position can seldom afford the luxury of that kind of emotion.

Hoffer and Burke had moved to a small illuminated patio where another fountain that was an exact duplicate of the first lifted into the night. They were sitting at a wrought-iron table and rose to greet me.

Hoffer had the kind of out-of-season tan that usually means a lamp or, more rarely, someone rich enough to follow the sun. On closer acquaintance, he was older than I had imagined, his face a network of fine seams, and in spite of the ready smile his eyes were cold and opaque.

We shook hands and he waved me to a seat. "Sorry I wasn't here when you got in. I'm having to run down to Gela three or four times a week now. You know the oil game."

I didn't, but I remembered Gela, a Greek colony in classic times, mainly as a pleasant little coastal town on the other side of the island with some interesting archaeological remains. I wondered how the derricks and refineries were fitting in and accepted a large vodka and tonic from Rosa.

She dismissed the houseboy and served us herself, dropping unobtrusively into a chair in the background when she had finished, which seemed to indicate that Hoffer trusted her all the way—something I'd been wrong about.

He certainly didn't waste any time in getting down to business. "Mr. Wyatt, Colonel Burke recommended you highly for this job, which is why we went to so much trouble to get you out."

"That was real nice of him," I said and the irony was in my voice for all to hear.

Except Hoffer, apparently, who carried on. "In fact I don't think it's overdoing it to say that we're all depending on you, boy."

He put his hand on my knee, which I didn't like, and there was the sort of edge to his voice that you get with the kind of American wheat-belt politician who's trying to persuade you he's just folks after all. Any minute now I expected him to break into a chorus of "I believe in you" and I couldn't have that.

"Let's get one thing straight, Mr. Hoffer. I'm here for

twenty-five thousand dollars plus expenses in advance."

He straightened abruptly, the head went back, the eyes hardened into chips of blue glass. I expected him to argue about the terms, because Burke actually looked alarmed and moved in fast.

"I'm sorry about this, Mr. Hoffer. Stacey doesn't realise . . ."

Hoffer cut him off with a motion of one hand that was like a sword falling. "Never mind. I like a man who knows his own mind. So long as we all know where we stand."

He was another man—hard, competent with the kind of ruthless edge he would have needed to get where he was. Even his physical movements were different. He snapped his fingers for another drink and Rosa Solazzo came running.

"Half in advance," he said. "To you and Burke."

"And if we fail to get the girl out?"

"You're that much ahead of the game."

"And the other two?"

"Your affair."

Burke was frowning, mainly, I suppose, because he felt he was being cut out of things. He nodded slightly, which surprised me—or did it really?

In any event I shook my head and said to Hoffer, "Not good enough. Jaeger and Legrande get the same terms or we don't go."

He didn't even argue. "All right. I'll let you have a check you can draw in Palermo tomorrow, but made out to Colonel Burke. He holds the bank until the job is over one way or the other. Some insurance for me against anyone preferring a bird in the hand."

"Fair enough."

Burke was obviously furiously angry, but I ignored him and emptied my glass. Rosa came over to get me another. Hoffer said, "Can we get down to business now? How do you intend to tackle this thing?"

"You're certain Serafino is in the Cammarata?" I said.

He nodded. "That definitely seems to be his home ground. Every inquiry I've been able to make confirms it. You know the area, I believe?"

"I've been there. It's wild country."

"You don't need to tell me. I had to drive up there alone to make the first payment."

"And you met him?"

"Serafino?" He nodded. "Face-to-face at a bridge on what passes for the main road near a village called Bellona."

"What was he like?"

"I can show you." He produced a wallet, took out a photo and gave it to me. "I got that through someone I know in the police. Our friend has been through their hands more than once."

It was typical of police photography the world over, reducing the subject to a kind of Neanderthal man, capable —from his appearance—of rape or murder and most things in between.

I shook my head. "This doesn't tell me a thing. What was he like? Describe him."

"Twenty-five or -six—medium height. Dark hair—long dark hair." He didn't approve of that. "One of those swarthy faces you get round here—they tell me it's the Arab blood from Saracen days. Typical Sicilian."

"Sounds just like me," I said.

"If you like." He wasn't in the least put out. "He's lost an eye since the photo was taken and he laughed a lot. Treated the whole thing as if it was one big joke."

And he hadn't liked that either. His right hand clenched into a fist and stayed that way. "I think Bellona sounds like a good place to start," I said.

Hoffer seemed surprised. "Is that such a good idea? The impression I get is that most of the villagers in the area work hand in glove with people like Serafino."

I looked at Burke. "You play the tourist. I'll pass myself off as a hire-car driver."

He nodded. "Suits me."

I turned to Hoffer. "Not the Mercedes. Something that isn't too ostentatious. Can you manage that?"

"Certainly. Is there anything else you'd like?"

"Yes, tell me about the girl."

He looked slightly bewildered. "Joanna? But I thought the colonel told you all you needed to know."

"I'd like to hear about her from you—all about her In a thing like this it's important to know as much as you can about people. That way you can have some ideas in advance about how they might behave in a given situation."

He was full of approval. "That makes sense. All right— where should I begin?"

"When you first met her would do for a start."

Which was when she was twelve years old. Her father had died of leukemia two years earlier. Hoffer had met her and the mother at San Moritz one Christmas and the marriage had taken place shortly afterwards and had lasted until four month previously when his wife had been killed in a car crash in France.

"I understand the girl was rather a handful," I said. "Presumably her mother's death didn't help."

He seemed to slump wearily, ran a hand across his face and sighed. "Where do you begin with a thing like this? Look, Wyatt, I'll put it in a nutshell for you When Joanna was fourteen her mother found her in bed with the chauffeur and he wasn't the first. She's been nothing but trouble ever since—one rotten little scandal after another."

"Then why are you bothering?"

He looked surprised, then frowned as if it hadn't occurred to him before. "A good question—certainly not because of any great affection. She's no good, she never has been and I honestly don't think she ever will be. Maybe it isn't her fault, but that's the way it is. No, I suppose when it all comes down to it I owe it to my wife. She was a wonderful woman. The seven years she gave me were the best, Wyatt. Anything else can only be afters."

He certainly sounded sincere and the presence of Rosa Solazzo didn't alter my judgment in the slightest. I was certainly the last man in the world to hold the fact that he needed a woman around against him.

"One thing puzzles me," I said. "I can understand you not going near the police. In Sicily they are worse than useless in a case like this, but didn't it ever occur to you to approach Mafia?"

"What good would that do?" Burke laughed. "Stacey has this Mafia thing on the brain, Mr. Hoffer. There are reasons."

Hoffer waved him down. "Sure I tried Mafia. They're still behind most things here. Don't believe all this crap you hear about Rome having stamped it out. That's just for the tourist trade. They don't want to scare anyone away."

"Did you get anywhere?"

He shook his head. "It seems Serafino Lentini doesn't like the Mafia. The impression I got was that they'd like to get their hands on him, too."

"Stacey's grandfather is something to do with this Mafia thing," Burke said. "Isn't that so, Stacey? He's going to see him tonight."

Hoffer frowned. "Your grandfather?"

"Vito Barbaccia," I said, I think for effect more than anything.

Rosa Solazzo sucked in her breath and dropped her glass. Hoffer stared at me incredulously in the following silence. "You are Vito Barbaccia's grandson?"

"You've heard of him, I take it?"

"Heard of him? Who hasn't? And you are seeing him tonight?"

I nodded and he shook his head. "I can't get over it."

"You've met him?" Burke asked.

Hoffer smiled. "Twice—at parties, but never to speak to. Only Royalty gets that close."

Burke looked at me, a frown on his face and I realised that everything I had told him at the cemetery hadn't really registered, certainly not the fundamental fact of just how important my grandfather was.

I drained my glass and got to my feet. "Well, I think I'll take a turn round the garden before dinner."

"Why not?" Hoffer nodded to Rosa. "Show him the sights, angel. There's a fish pond round the back that's quite a showpiece, Mr. Wyatt."

Now he was calling me Mr. again. Strange how the Barbaccia affected people. And Rosa? Rosa had gone very pale and when I smiled at her she dropped her gaze, fear in those dark eyes.

Barbaccia—*mafioso*. I suppose that to her the two were interchangeable. When I tucked her arm in mine, she was trembling.

Hoffer obviously used a first-rate local chef. We had *narbe di San Paolo*, which is a kind of ravioli filled with sugar and ricotta cheese and fried, and *cannoli*, probably the most famous sweet in Sicily, consisting of a tube of flour and egg filled with cream. The others drank Marsala, which is too sweet for me, and I had a bottle of Zibibbo from the island of Pantelleria, a wine which is flavoured with anise. The sort of thing you either like at once or not at all.

We dined on the terrace, a rather conventional little group, with Piet and Legrande very much on their best behaviour. Later—the wine having taken effect—things livened up a little. Piet gave all his attention to Rosa, though strictly at a superficial level, and even Legrande unwound enough to smile once or twice.

The coffee was Yemeni *mocha*, probably the best in the

world. I took mine to the edge of the terrace to drink. The laughter was louder now and no one appeared to notice as I faded away.

I went up to my room, got the Smith & Wesson in its spring holster from the drawer and snapped it to my belt. I pulled it clear a couple of times to make sure things were working all right and Burke came in. He closed the door and leaned against it.

"Expecting trouble?"

"I'm not sure."

I replaced the Smith & Wesson, buttoned my jacket and slipped half a dozen spare rounds into my lefthand pocket and Marco's Walther in the right.

"I'd like to come with you," he said. "It might help."

I looked him straight in the eye and he held my gaze, grave and serious. I nodded. "If you like."

He smiled in a kind of relief—he was doing a lot of smiling these days—and slapped me on the shoulder. "The old firm, eh, Stacey boy?"

But it could never be that again, nothing was more certain.

7

MONTE PELLEGRINO, which is about three miles to the north of Palermo, towers into the sky at the western end of the Conca d'Oro. It's an interesting place, soaked in blood and history like the rest of Sicily. During the Punic Wars, Hamilcar Barca held it against the Romans for three years, but in more modern times it became famous mainly because of the cult of Santa Rosalia, after whom my mother had been named. My grandfather's villa was at the foot of the mountain just outside the village of Valdesi.

I suppose, when you thought about it, he'd come a long way. He was born in Velba, a village in western Sicily which was depressingly typical of the region, a dung heap where most children died in their first year and life was roughly equivalent to what it had been in England in mediaeval times.

His father was a share-cropper and the living that gave was of a kind that barely maintained life. Of his early years I knew little for certain, but by the time he was twenty-three he was a *gabellotto*, a mixture of tax collector and land agent whose function was to screw the sharecroppers down and keep them that way.

Only a *mafioso* could have the job, so he was on the way up at an early age. God knows what had happened in between—a killing or two—perhaps more, which was the usual method for any youngster to make his way in the Honoured Society.

He might even have spent some time as a *sicario*, a hired killer, but I doubted that. It didn't fit into the code—his own very individual conception of what was honourable and what was not. The idea of making money out of prostitution, for example, filled him with horror because he believed in the sanctity of the family and gave to the Church. On the other hand, the organisation he served had killed so many of its opponents over the years that in many towns murder was a commonplace.

The lights of the car picked out a couple of old women trudging towards us festooned with baskets.

"What in the hell was that supposed to be?" Burke demanded.

"They're coming in for tomorrow's market."

"At this time of night?"

"The only way they can secure a good pitch."

He shook his head. "What a bloody country."

I looked into the night at the lights of the city. "That's one Sicily, but out there in the darkness is another. A charnel house for generations. The breadbasket of the Roman Empire based completely on slave labour. Ever since then the people have been exploited by someone or other."

"I didn't really take it all in," he said. "This Mafia stuff. I though it was all in the past."

"I can think of one place that's had better than a hundred and fifty killings in four years—a town of less than twenty thousand inhabitants. You won't find me a place in the world of comparable size that can match that."

"But why?" he said. "I just don't get it."

"People play games of one sort or another all the time, haven't you ever noticed that?"

"I don't follow you."

I could have told him that he'd been playing soldiers all his life—even in the Congo—but there would have been no point. He wouldn't have understood what I was talking about and I'd have offended him needlessly.

"Let me put it this way. In the suburbs of Los Angeles or London, the struggle to keep abreast of the next man, the cut and thrust of business or even an affair with someone else's wife, adds that little touch of drama to life that everyone needs."

"And what does that prove?"

"Nothing in particular. In Sicily it's an older game, that's all, and rather more savage. The ritual of *vendetta* —an eye for an eye, neither more nor less. And the rules may seem a little barbaric to outsiders. We kiss the wounds of our dead, touch our lips to the blood and say: In this way may I drink the blood of the one who killed you."

Even thinking of it touched something inside me—a coldness like a snake uncoiling.

"You said we," Burke observed. "You include yourself in?"

I stared out into the distance where an early cruise ship passed beyond the headland, a blaze of lights, a world of its own. I thought of school in London at St. Paul's, of Wyatt's Landing, of Harvard and laughed.

"In any village in Sicily if I spoke my grandfather's name and declared my relationship, there would be men who would kiss my hand. You're in another world here, Sean, try to get that into your head."

But I don't think he believed me—not then. It all seemed too improbable. Belief would come later.

There was no resemblance at all between the Barbaccia villa and Hoffer's place. To start with, the walls were at least two thousand years older, for like most country houses it had been built on a Roman site. They were about fifteen feet high and the villa itself was of Moorish origin and stood in the centre of a couple of acres of semi-tropical garden. Ciccio braked to a halt and sounded his horn.

The gatekeeper wasn't armed, but then he didn't need to be. A man appeared from the lodge behind him wrestling with two bull mastiffs of a breed common to the island since Norman times and another came out of the bushes holding a machine pistol.

The gatekeeper wore a neat khaki uniform and looked more like an insurance clerk with his moustache and steel-rimmed spectacles. There was a kind of impasse while he and his friends stared at us and the dogs didn't bark, which was somehow even more sinister.

I opened the door, got out and approached. "I'm expected," I said. "You must have been told."

"One man, signor, not three. No car passes through these gates except the *capo's*. A rule of the house."

I produced the Walther very carefully from my pocket and there was a hollow click as the gentleman with the machine pistol cocked it. I passed the Walther through the bars, butt first.

"My calling card. Send it to Marco—Marco Gagini. He'll tell you who I am."

He shrugged. "All right, you can come in, but the others stay outside with the car."

Marco came round the bend of the drive on the run and slowed to a halt. He stared past me at the Mercedes, at Burke and Ciccio, then nodded. "Open the gates—let them in."

The gatekeeper started to protest. "You know the rule —only house cars allowed inside."

Marco shook him by the lapel. "Fool, does a man kill his own grandfather? Get out of the way."

He wrenched the Walther from the gatekeeper's hand,

dropped it into his pocket and pushed him towards the lodge. The gates, it seemed, were electronically controlled. They swung back with a slight whisper and Marco joined us.

"I'll ride up to the house with you."

We got into the rear beside Burke and Ciccio drove on slowly. "Things have changed," I said to Marco. "Getting into Fort Knox would be easier."

"An electronic device runs round the top of the walls," he told me seriously. "So no one can get in that way. Usually, as you just heard, cars other than our own aren't allowed through. We discovered an explosive device in one a few years back when the *capo* was giving a party. If it had gone off it would have taken the villa with it."

"A nice way to live."

Perhaps the irony in my voice escaped him or else he chose to ignore it. "There have been eight attempts on the *capo's* life in the last few years. We have to be very careful. Who is this man you have brought with you?" he added in exactly the same tone.

"A friend of mine—Colonel Burke. He thought I might need some help."

"I can feel the gun in his pocket. Most uncomfortable. Tell him it will not be needed."

"I know enough Italian to understand that much," Burke said and transferred his Browning to the other pocket.

The Mercedes halted at the bottom of a broad flight of steps that lifted to a great oaken door banded with iron which I'd always understood had had an arrow or two in it in its day.

I think that until that moment nothing had possessed any reality for me. I was home again, which was what it came down to, and it was as if some part of me, some essential part, simply didn't want to know.

Burke followed me out and Marco told Ciccio to take

the Mercedes round to the courtyard at the rear. It
moved away smoothly, I turned and found my grandfather
standing at the top of the steps.

He was as large as Burke and looked smaller only because his shoulders were stooped a little with age. At that
time he must have been sixty-seven or -eight and yet
there was still colour in the long hair and carefully trimmed
beard.

If I say he had the look of a Roman Emperor, I would
be referring to the period when it was possible for a rest-
less adventurer with no scruples to rise from the ranks.

It was a remarkable face. There was ruthlessness there,
and arrogance, but also pride and a blazing intelligence.
And he was as elegant as ever. Many of the old-time *capo
mafias* chose to look as slovenly and as unkempt as possible in society as if to emphasise their power and importance, but not Vito Barbaccia. The share-cropper's son
had left his rags behind him long ago.

He wore a cream lightweight suit that had London
stamped all over it, a pink shirt and dark blue silk tie. The
cigar was as large as ever and the ebony walking stick I
remembered well, because if it was the same one, it housed
a couple of feet of razor-sharp steel.

He didn't speak as I went slowly up the steps to meet
him. I paused a little below his level and he gazed down
at me, still without a word, and then his arms opened.

The strength was still there. He held me close for a
long moment, then gave me the ritual kiss on each cheek
and pushed me at arm's length.

"You've grown, Stacey—you've grown, boy."

I motioned to Burke, who came up the steps, and I in-
troduced them. My voice seemed to belong to a stranger,
to come from far away under water and my eyes were hot.
He sensed my distress, squeezed my arm and tucked it
into his own.

I refused to be drawn. "That would be about two years ago now."

"What have you been up to since?"

"This and that." I went towards him, a goblet in each hand. "As a matter of fact I'm just out of prison. The Egyptian variety. Nothing like as pleasant as the Ucciardone in Palermo or doesn't the Mafia control it any more?"

The ebony stick stabbed out, sweeping back my coat, exposing the Smith & Wesson in its holster. "So, Marco was right and I wouldn't believe him. This is what you have become, eh? *Sicario*—hired killer. My grandson."

Strange the anger in his voice, the disgust, but then no real *mafioso* ever thought of himself as a criminal. Everything was for the cause, for the Society.

I handed him his brandy. "Am I worse than you? In any way am I worse than you?"

"When I kill, it is in hot blood," he said. "A man dies because he is against me—against Mafia."

"And you think that sufficient reason?"

He shrugged. "I believe it to be so. It has always been so." The stick came up and touched my chest. "But you, Stacey, what do you kill for? Money?"

"Not just money," I said. "Lots of money."

Which wasn't true. I knew it and I think he did also.

"I can give you money. All you need."

"That's just what you did for a great many years."

"And you left."

"And I left."

He nodded gravely. "I had a letter from some lawyers in the States just over a year ago. They were trying to trace you. Your grandfather—old Wyatt—had second thoughts on his death bed. There is provision for you in the will—a large sum."

I wasn't even angry. "They can give it back to the Indians."

"You won't touch it?"

"Would I walk on my mother's grave?" I was getting more like a Sicilian every minute.

He seemed well pleased. "I am glad to see you have some honour left in you. Now you will tell me why you are here. I do not flatter myself that you returned to Sicily to see me."

I crossed the room and poured another brandy. "Bread and butter work—nothing to interest you."

The stick hammered on the floor. "I asked you a question, boy, you will answer."

"All right. If it will make you feel any better. Burke and I have been hired by a man named Hoffer."

"Karl Hoffer?" He frowned slightly.

"That's the man. Austrian, but speaks English like an American. Has interests in the oilfield at Gela."

"I know what his interests are. What does he want you to do?"

"I thought Mafia knew everything," I said. "His stepdaughter was kidnapped some weeks ago by a bandit called Serafino Lentini. He's holding her in the Cammarata and won't send her back in spite of the fact that Hoffer paid up like a soldier."

"And you are going to get her back, is that it? You and your friend think you can go into the Cammarata and bring her out with you again?" He laughed, that strange, harsh laugh, head thrown back. "Stacey—Stacey. And I thought you'd grown up."

I very carefully smashed my crystal goblet into the fire, and started for the door. His voice, when he called my name, had all the iron of hell in it. I turned, a twelve-year-old schoolboy again caught in the orange grove before harvest. "That was seventeenth-century Florentine. Does it make you feel any better?"

I shook my head. "I'm sorry."

There was nothing more I could say. Unexpectedly he

smiled. "This Serafino Lentini—you are kin on your grandmother's side. Third cousins."

"You know him then?"

"I haven't seen him for many years. A wild boy—he shot a policeman when he was eighteen and took to the *maquis*. When they caught him, they gave him a hard time. You've heard of the *cassetta?*"

In the good old days under Mussolini it had been frequently employed by the police when extorting confessions from the more difficult prisoners. A kind of wooden box, a frame to which a man could be strapped and worked on at leisure. It was supposed to be forbidden now, but whether it was or not was anyone's guess.

"What did they do to him?"

"The usual things—the hot iron, which left him blind in one eye, and they crushed his testicles—took away his manhood."

Burke should be listening to this. "Does nothing change?" I said.

"Nothing." He shook his head. "And watch Hoffer. He is a hard man."

"Millionaires usually are. That's how they get there." I buttoned my jacket. "It's time I was going. A long day tomorrow."

"You are going to the Cammarata?"

I nodded. "With Burke. Just for a drive. Tourists having a look around. I want to see the lay of the land. I thought we'd try Bellona."

"The man who owns the wineshop is the mayor. His name is Cerda—Danielo Cerda." He took his blue silk handkerchief from his breast pocket and held it out. "Show him this and tell him you are from me. He will help you in any way he can. He is one of my people."

I folded the handkerchief and put it in my pocket. "I thought Serafino didn't like Mafia."

"He doesn't," he said tranquilly, reached for my hand

and pulled himself up. "Now we shall join the others. I must talk with this Colonel Burke of yours. He interests me."

Burke and Marco were sitting together in the salon, an exquisite room which my grandfather had kept to the original Moorish design. The floor was of black and white ceremic tiles and the ceiling was blue, vivid against stark white walls. Beyond a wonderful carved screen, another relic of Saracen days, was the terrace and the gardens.

I could hear water gurgling in the old conduits, splashing from the numerous fountains. In other days it had been said that whoever held the meager water supplies of the island held Sicily, and Mafia had done just that.

They were talking behind me and I heard Burke say in his terrible Italian, "You must be very proud of your garden, Signor Barbaccia."

"The best in Sicily," my grandfather told him. "Come, I will show you."

Marco stayed to finish his drink and I followed them out onto the terrace. The sky was clear again, each star a jewel and the lush, semi-tropical vegetation pressed in on the house.

I could smell the orange grove although I couldn't see it, the almond trees. Palms swayed gently in the slight breeze, their branches dark feathers against the stars. And everywhere the gurgle of water. My grandfather pointed out the papyrus by the pool, another Arab innovation, and suggested a short walk before we left.

He moved towards the steps leading down to the garden, Burke paused to light a cigarette and then everything happened at once.

Some instinct, product perhaps of the years of hard living, sent a wave of coldness through me and I froze, ready to jump like some jungle animal sensing an unseen presence.

Below the steps five yards on the other side of the gravel

path, the leaves trembled and a gun barrel poked through. My grandfather was already on his way down. I sent him sprawling with a stiff left arm, drew and fired three times. A machine pistol jumped into the air, there was a kind of choking cough and a man fell out of the bushes and rolled onto his back.

I dropped to one knee beside my grandfather. "Are you all right?"

"There will be another," he said calmly.

"Hear that, Sean?" I called.

"I'll cover you," came the reply in a voice like ice-water. "Roust him out."

Marco came through the french windows in a hurry, the Walther in his hand, and a shotgun blasted from the bushes over to my right, too far away to do any damage. You have to be close with those things. Marco dropped from view and I took a running jump into the greenery.

I landed badly, rolled over twice and came up about six feet away from number two. He was clutching a sawn-off shotgun in both hands, the *lupara,* traditional weapon used in a Mafia ritual killing.

I took one hell of a chance, simply because it seemed like a good idea to keep him in one piece to talk, and fired as I came up, catching him in the left arm. He screamed and dropped the *lupara.* Not that it did much good. As he straightened and backed away, Burke shot him between the eyes from the terrace.

He looked about seventeen, a boy trying to make a name for himself, to gain respect—the kind Mafia often used for this kind of work. The other was a different breed, a real pro from the look of him, with hard, bitter eyes fixed in death.

My grandfather pushed the jacket aside with his stick and said to Marco, "You told me he could use a gun. Look at that."

I'd shot him three times in the heart, the holes covering

no more than the width of two fingers between them.
There was very little blood. I could hear the mastiffs bark-
ing and the guards arrived as I reloaded and slipped the
Smith & Wesson back into its holster.

"How did they get in?"

The old man frowned and turned to Marco. "How
about that? You told me this place was impregnable."

Marco motioned to the guards without a word and they
went off in a hurry, dogs and all. I stirred the man on the
ground with my foot.

"So, they're still trying?"

"Not for much longer," he said grimly. "I can assure
you. All bills will be paid. I owe it to your mother."

I was shaken, but I turned to Burke. "That's Mafia for
you. Just one big happy family. Will there be any trouble
over these two?"

My grandfather shook his head. "I'll have the police
come and take them away."

"As simple as that?"

"But of course. It would, however, be wiser if you
were to leave before they get here."

He called to Marco, who was rooting around out there
in the garden somewhere, to send the Mercedes round,
then took me by the arm and walked a little way off.

"If you could play the piano like you can shoot,
Stacey . . ."

"A shame, isn't it?" I said. "But my mother was right
about one thing. We all have a talent for something."

He sighed. "Go with God, boy. Come and see me when
you get back from the Cammarata, eh?"

"I'll do that."

"I'll expect you." He turned and held out his hand.
"Colonel, my thanks."

Later, after we had passed through the gates, Burke lit
another cigarette and when the match flared I saw sweat

on his face. I wondered if he had been afraid, but that didn't seem possible.

"Are you all right?" I asked.

At first I thought I wasn't going to get a reply and then it came, delivered with some bitterness. "Christ knows what they did to you in that place you were in, but it must have been bad."

He was at last facing the fact that I had changed, really changed, which suited me perfectly. I sat there looking out to sea, thinking, not of what had just happened at the villa, but of Karl Hoffer and the Honourable Joanna and Serafino Lentini, the great lover who desired her so much that he insisted on keeping her just for himself. Serafino who had lost his manhood, according to my grandfather, under police torture and was incapable of the physical act of love.

Now why had Vito Barbaccia, *capo mafia*, arch schemer, gone out of his way to tell me that?

8

HOFFER was as good as his word and provided a Fiat saloon for the reconnaissance trip. He also threw in Rosa Solazzo for good measure. His argument was that, being a woman, she would provide good cover and strengthen our story, but I suspected she was there to look after his interests as much as anything.

The final meeting on the following morning was a hurried one. He was flying to Catania on business in the Cessna and wanted to be away early so that he could be back that evening to hear what I thought about the situation on our return.

No mention was made of the shooting match at the villa, something else I found interesting. On the way back Burke had asked me to keep it to myself and seemed to think that it might upset a respectable businessman like Hoffer to be associated with that kind of violence. But Ciccio had been there and must have heard the shooting at the very least, although he had been his usual phlegmatic self on the way back. I found it hard to believe that he hadn't passed on news of the disturbance.

The route we followed was one normally taken by

tourists driving across the island to Agrigento, certainly those in search of spectacular scenery. I did the driving as originally planned, Burke sat beside me and Rosa Solazzo had the rear seat to herself.

She looked very attractive in a navy blue trouser suit cut on rather mannish lines, off-set by a more than feminine ruffled blouse in white nylon. A red silk scarf bound round her head peasant-fashion completed the outfit, plus, of course, the ever-present sunglasses.

She didn't attempt to make conversation and read a magazine. When I stopped at the village of Misilmeri about ten miles out to buy cigarettes and asked if she wanted anything, her only reply was a shake of the head.

Obviously her presence limited conversation between Burke and myself, but in any case he didn't seem much in the mood and slouched back in his seat, sombre and brooding as if carrying the weight of the world, and there was that slight tremble in his hands again.

For the first time I found myself wondering whether he was up to what lay ahead. On the other hand, he'd shown no sign of having slowed down any during the affair at the villa. The shot which had killed the boy with the *lupara* had been a difficult one and yet he had been right on the button. Having said that, early warning signs of some kind of deterioration showed clearly and they didn't look good. For the time being I pushed it out of my mind and concentrated on enjoying the trip.

It was almost the end of spring harvest, orange groves ripening in the warm air and flowers everywhere. Red poppies, anemones and, in some places, blue iris spread like a carpet into the distance. Another week and the iron hand of summer would grasp the land by the throat and squeeze it dry, leaving in the high country a wilderness of thirst, a gaunt North African land of rock and sand and lava.

The farther we moved away from Palermo into the

heart of things, the more I realized how little it had changed. Out here one didn't see the three-wheeler Lambrettas and Vespas so common in the farming area immediately adjacent to Palermo. Here, one moved through a mediaeval landscape, through poverty of a kind to be found in few places in Europe.

We passed an old peasant riding a donkey, a little farther on a line of gaunt women, baskets on their heads, dressed in fusty black as if mourning their very existence, skirts trailing in the dust, who turned brown, seamed faces to watch us pass, old before their time.

And the villages seemed just the same, most of the houses windowless, the door the only source of light and air, opening into a dark cavern that housed, in many cases, pigs and goats as well as people.

And in the villages, mainly women, old men and thin, hungry-looking children, living out their lives against a dying landscape.

In one such place, I stopped outside a small *trattoria* and we sat at a rough wooden table in the shade and the proprietor, an old, old man with white hair, brought a bottle of *passito,* ice-cold from the bottom of his well.

It was about eleven o'clock, but already very warm and when a ring of solemn-faced children surrounded us we could smell the sourness of their unwashed bodies.

"Don't they have any men around here?" Burke demanded.

He looked tired and was sweating a lot, great damp patches soaking his shirt beneath each arm. "Most of them have emigrated," I told him. "I've heard it said that in some provinces eighty-five per cent of the population is made up of women and children."

He looked disgusted and wiped sweat from his forehead. "What a bloody country."

Rosa Solazzo had disappeared into the back to find whatever passed for a toilet in those parts and rejoined us in time to hear his comment. She obviously didn't approve.

"This is one of the poorest areas in Europe, Colonel Burke. In summer it has the same climate as North Africa, the land is barely cultivatable and what water there is, is controlled by the Mafia. These people are born without hope. What else can they do, but try and get out?"

Not that she had a hope in hell of making him understand. The people she was speaking of were her people—she was one of them, had probably started life in just such a place as this.

Burke laughed with a kind of contempt. "You seem to be doing all right, anyway."

She pushed her way through the children and got into the Fiat. I emptied my glass and shook my head as Burke poured himself another. "I wouldn't if I were you. Strong stuff, *passito*."

That was enough, of course, to make him fill the glass to the brim. I left him there and got behind the wheel again. I found my cigarettes and offered one to Rosa.

"I'm sorry about that. He doesn't understand."

She was bitterly angry. "I don't need your regrets. At least he only speaks from ignorance, but you and your kind—you and Mafia—are responsible for most of this."

So, I was still *mafioso*? I turned away and she leaned across and touched me on the shoulder. "No, I am angry with him and I place it on you. You will forgive me?"

I couldn't tell what was going on behind the dark glasses. Did she imagine she had gone too far and was trying to recover her ground, or was she afraid at the very thought of offending Vito Barbaccia's grandson? Or was it at all possible that she was just sorry?

My answer amply fitted every contingency. "That's all right."

Burke was on his third large glass. He finished it, stood up and sat down abruptly, looking surprised.

"You warned him about *passito*?" Rosa asked.

"He isn't in the mood for advice."

She started to laugh. Revenge, particularly where women are concerned, is always sweet.

We moved into the high country now, the great craggy solitudes around Monte Cammarata, the mountain itself towering almost six thousand feet into the sky.

Burke had lapsed into a kind of stupor and Rosa leaned her arms on the back of my seat and we talked softly, our voices dropping a degree or two as the crags closed in around us.

We turned off the main road, zig-zagging up into the hills, the valley deepening beneath us. A hell of a country, home of runaway slaves and bandits since Roman times.

During the war this had been the most strategic point in the Italian-German defence system when the Allies invaded the island and yet the Americans had passed through unheeded, thanks, it was said, to the fact that most of the Italian troops had deserted after a Mafia directive.

The road narrowed, but we had it all to ourselves and I kept close to the wall, climbing slowly in second gear in a cloud of dust. The only living things we saw were a shepherd and his flock high up above a line of beech trees and then we rounded a shoulder and found Bellona a hundred yards away.

For many years, because of the constant state of anarchy and banditry in rural Sicily, the people have tended to congregate in villages much larger than are found elsewhere in Europe. Bellona was smaller than most, although that was probably to be expected in the sparsely populated high country.

Several streets slanted down to a square, mostly open sewers if the stench of urine was anything to go by, and thin children played listlessly in the dirt.

I pulled up outside the wineshop. There were three wooden tables with benches placed in the shade and two men sat drinking red wine. One of them was old, a typical peasant in shiny dark suit. His companion was a different breed, a short, thick-set man of forty or so with the kind of face that doesn't tan and dark, deep-set eyes.

Something makes a *mafioso*, the peculiar stare, the air of authority, a kind of detachment from other men. This man was Cerda, I was certain of that as he got to his feet and moved to the car.

"What can I do for you, signor?" he asked as I got out to meet him.

Burke was by now looking really ill. Great beads of sweat oozed from his face and he had a hand screwed tightly into his stomach.

"We're on our way to Agrigento," I said. "One of my passengers has been taken ill." He leaned down and looked at Burke and then Rosa and I added, "Are you the proprietor?"

He nodded. "What is he, American?"

"Irish. He put away a bottle of *passito* at the last stop. Wouldn't be told."

"Tourists." He shook his head. "We'll get him inside."

I said to Rosa, "Better to wait out here, signorina. Can I get you anything?"

She hesitated, then smiled slightly. "Coffee and make certain they boil the water."

"I'll send my wife out at once, signorina," Cerda said. "Perhaps you would care to sit at one of the tables?"

She got out of the car as we took Burke in between us. There was a cracked marble bar, half-a-dozen tables and a passage beyond. Cerda kicked open a door and we went into a small, cluttered bedroom, obviously his own. We eased Burke on to the bed and I loosened his tie.

"A couple of hours and he'll be over the worst," Cerda said. "A hell of a hangover, but he'll be able to travel. I'll be back in a minute."

He left, presumably to arrange about the coffee, and I

lit a cigarette and went to the window. A minute or so later the door clicked open again and when I turned he was leaning against it, a hand behind his back.

"And now we talk. Who are you?"

"You're quick," I said.

He shook his head. "No one in his right mind on the way to Agrigento turns off to drive ten miles over the worst road in Sicily for fun."

"You're right, of course. I'm going to take something out of my right-hand pocket so don't shoot me. It isn't a gun."

The handkerchief had roughly the same effect as a holy relic. I thought, for a moment, that he was going to kiss it. He took an old Colt .45 automatic from behind his back, probably a relic of the war, and put it down on top of a chest of drawers.

"So, you are from the *capo?* I felt sure you were of the Society from the moment I saw you, but one can always be wrong. Strange that we have not met before. I'm in Palermo every month on business for the Society."

"I've been away for a few years. Just returned." I decided to give him all guns. "I'm the *capo's* grandson."

His eyes widened and for a moment I honestly thought he might genuflect. "But of course, I remember your mother, God rest her." He crossed himself. "An American father, that was it. I thought there was something not quite Sicilian about you. What about your friend?"

"He's working with me, but the story about the *passito* was true enough."

He grinned. "We'll leave him to it. Cooler in the kitchen, anyway."

It was a large square room with one small window so that it was in semi-darkness in spite of the bright sun outside. He brought a bottle of wine to the table, filled a couple of glasses and motioned me to sit. His wife flitted from the stove like a dark wraith, a tray in her hands, and vanished through the door.

"Now, what brings the *capo's* grandson to Bellona?"

"Serafino Lentini," I said.

He paused, his glass half-way to his lips, then lowered it again. "You'd like to get your hands on Serafino?" He laughed. "Mother of God, so would I. And the *capo* told you to see me? I don't understand. The Society has been after Serafino for nearly two years now. He's given us a lot of trouble and the people round here go for him in a big way." He swallowed some of his wine and sighed. "Very discouraging."

"What is he trying to be?" I said. "Another Giuliano— a Robin Hood?"

He spat on the floor. "Serafino's just like the rest of us, out for number one, but he does the shepherds a few favours from time to time or stops some old woman from being evicted, so they think the sun shines out of his backside. Six months ago near Frentini, he held up the local bus that was carrying wages to a co-operative, shot the driver, and a bank clerk. The driver died two days later."

"A real hard man," I commented.

"Wild," he said. "Never grown up. Mind you, he suffered greatly at the hands of the police when he was younger. Lost the sight of an eye. I personally think he's never got over it. But what do you want with him?"

I told him as much as he needed to know and when I was finished, he shook his head. "But this is madness. You could never hope to get anywhere near Serafino. Here, I will show you."

He opened a drawer and produced a large-scale survey map of the region. It showed the whole Monte Cammarata area in detail.

"Here is where Serafino is staying at the moment." He indicated a spot on the map on the other side of the mountain about fifteen hundred feet below the summit.

"There's a shepherd's hut up there beside a stream. He uses it all the time except when he's on the run."

I showed my surprise. "You're certain?"

He smiled sadly. "Let me tell you the facts of life. Knowing where Serafino is and catching him there are two different things. Every shepherd on the mountain worships him, every goatherd. They have a signalling system from crag to crag that informs him of the approach of anyone when they're still three or four hours' hard climbing away. I've tried to catch him with local men who belong to us—mountain men. We've always failed."

"How many men does he have with him?"

"At the moment, three. The Vivaldi brothers and Joe Ricco."

I examined the map for two or three minutes, then asked him to describe the area in detail. I didn't need to make notes, I'd done this sort of thing too often before.

In the end I nodded and folded the map. "Can I keep this?"

"Certainly. It's impossible, you realise that?"

"On the contrary." I smiled. "I feel rather more confident than I did earlier. Now I think I'll go for a walk. I'd like to have a look around. I'll see you later."

I paused in the street door, half-blinded by the sudden glare and put on my sunglasses. Rosa was seated at the wooden table nearest the car, a tray in front of her. She wasn't alone. The two specimens who lounged on the edge of the table were typical of the younger men still to be found in the region. Features brutalised and coarsened by a life of toil, shabby, patched clothing, broken boots, cloth caps that anywhere else in Europe belonged to another age.

Rosa's back was stiff and straight and she smoked a cigarette and stared into space. One of them said something, I couldn't catch what, and got what was left of her coffee in his face.

To a Sicilian male, a woman is there to be used, to do

what she is told. To be publicly humiliated by one would be unthinkable. Several of the watching children laughed and he reached across the table in a fury and yanked her to her feet, his other hand raised to strike.

I grabbed him by the shoulder and pulled him round. We stared at each other for a long moment and the expression on his face was already beginning to alter as I slapped him back-handed. I didn't say a word. His hand went to his cheek, his friend plucked at his sleeve. They walked backwards, faces blank, turned and hurried away.

Rosa joined me, buttoning her jacket. "What would you have done if they'd both had a go at you? Shot them?"

"But they didn't," I pointed out.

"No, you're right, they knew better than to tangle with Mafia."

"And how would they know that's what they were doing?"

"Don't play games with me, Mr. Wyatt. Have you looked in the mirror lately? There is *mafioso* stamped clear for all to see. The self-sufficiency, the power, the quiet arrogance. Why, you didn't even speak to that poor wretch. That was the most humiliating thing of all."

"For you or for him?" She raised a hand and I warded it off. "Poor Rosa. You wear nylon underwear and dresses from London and Paris and feel guilty about it. Why? Are there brothers and sisters still living in a sty like this?"

"Something like that." She nodded. "You are very clever, aren't you, Mr. Wyatt?"

"Stacey," I said. "Call me Stacey. Now let's take a walk."

Beyond the village we found a pleasant slope that lifted gently towards the first ridge-back, the dark line of forest beyond, then bare rock and the peak, very faint, shimmering in the heat haze.

I had brought binoculars from the car and I spread the

map Cerda had given me on the ground and carefully checked certain features with reality.

"Can it be done?" she asked as I folded the map and put the binoculars back into their case.

"I think so."

"But you're not going to tell me how?"

"I thought you only came along for the ride."

She hit me on the shoulder with a clenched fist. "I think you are the most infuriating man I have ever met."

"Good," I said. "Now let's forget everything else except how pleasant this is. We'll spend the afternoon like carefree lovers and tell pleasant lies to each other."

She laughed, head thrown back, but when I took her hand in mine, she let it stay there.

On the slopes we found knapweed with great yellow heads, ragwort and bee orchids and silvery-blue gentians. We walked for an hour, then lay in a hollow warmed by the sun, smoked and talked.

I was right. She had started life in a village very similar to Bellona in the province of Messina. An uncle on her mother's side, a widower, had owned a small cafe in Palermo and his only daughter had died. He needed someone to take her place in the business and no Sicilian would dream of bringing in an outsider when there was someone suitable in the family.

She had married at eighteen the middle-aged owner of a similar establishment who had obliged by conveniently passing on a year later.

My impression was that Hoffer had used the place and had taken a fancy to her, but she was a little reticent about the details. The important thing was that she'd been able to make herself into what he wanted, a sophisticated woman of the world, which couldn't have been easy, even with her guts and intelligence.

She fired a few questions at me in turn and I actually

found myself answering. Nothing important, of course, and then she slipped badly.

"It's incredible," she said. "You're almost human. It's so difficult to imagine you killing as ruthlessly as you did last night."

"So you know about that?" I said. "Who told you?"

"Why, Colonel Burke." The answer was out before she could stop it. "I was there when he told Karl."

Was anything ever going to make sense again? I laughed out loud and she asked me what was so funny.

"Life," I said. "One big joke."

I pushed her on her back and kissed her. She lay there staring up at me, her face smooth, the eyes quite blank, making no move to stop me as I unbuttoned her blouse and slipped a hand inside and cupped it around a breast. The nipple blossomed beneath my thumb and I noticed tiny beads of sweat on her brow.

I kissed them away and laughed. "There can be no doubt whatsoever that the trouser suit has been the greatest protector of a woman's virtue since the chastity belt. Almost an insoluble problem."

"But not quite," she said.

"No, not quite."

I kissed her again and this time her arms slid around my neck, pulling me close. She was really very desirable, but so untrustworthy.

We came down to the village a different way on our return and I got a look into the walled garden at the rear of the wineshop from a couple of hundred feet up. A red Alfa Romeo was parked in the barn and two men were talking in the entrance. When I got the binoculars out, I discovered it was Cerda and Marco Gagini.

Rosa had walked on ahead some little way, picking wild flowers. I didn't say anything to her, or indeed to Cerda when we returned to the wineshop. Burke was on his feet again by then, looking and acting pretty foul. I put him into the rear seat for the return trip and Rosa sat beside me.

He controlled his temper for at least a hundred yards and then exploded. "Well, aren't you going to tell me, for Christ's sake? What did you find?"

"Where Serafino hangs out."

"And we can get at him?"

"I think so. Remember the mission at Lagona?"

"Where we parachuted in for the nuns?" He frowned. "That's what you're suggesting now?"

"It's the only way," I said. "Can you get the gear together?"

He nodded. "No difficulty there. I'll have it flown in tomorrow from Crete. Look, are you sure about this?"

"I'll give it to you word by word when we get back," I told him. "Now why don't you try to get some more sleep?"

He laughed sourly. "Sleep? I'll never sleep again."

He subsided into the corner and I swung the Fiat into the first bend and came out in a cloud of dust. When I glanced into the mirror I was smiling.

We reached Palermo just before evening and there was one more thing to be done before we returned to the villa, as I reminded Burke. We called at Hoffer's bank, presented his check and had it converted to a Bill of Exchange to be drawn upon a firm of Swiss merchant bankers I designated. We left it on deposit in the bank vault from which it could be retrieved on presentation of a key they gave us plus his signature.

Burke wasn't pleased at all, mainly because I'd pushed him into it and he never liked that. The clerk gave me a large manilla envelope to put the Bill of Exchange in and I let Burke seal it, which seemed to make him feel a little better. I told him he could hang on to the key and he put it carefully away in his wallet.

For some reason he still didn't look really happy. I was rather pleased about that.

9

WHEN WE reached the villa, Hoffer hadn't returned.
Rosa disappeared to take a bath, which was exactly what
I wanted to do, but Burke seemed to come to life again.

"You'd better have some coffee and a shower before
Hoffer comes back," I told him. "If he sees you like this
he'll start worrying about his investment."

It had an effect of sorts. "To hell with Hoffer. He needs
me and he bloody well knows it. Now let's have words. I
want to know what you found up there today."

I humoured him to the extent of following him out
through the lounge to the terrace. Piet and Legrande were
sitting at a table playing cards, a bottle of something between them.

Piet jumped to his feet at once as Burke arrived, that
inner glow on his face again. "Thank God!" Legrande said.
"It's been as lively as a graveyard around here today. When
do we see some action?"

"Soon enough." Burke found time to smile at Piet and
squeezed his arm. "Bring us some coffee, there's a good
lad, and we'll get down to business."

Piet went out on the double and Burke took his chair,

put the tray with its bottles and glasses on the floor and looked up at me. "All right, Stacey, let's have it."

I unfolded the map Cerda had given me and spread it across the table. First of all I went through my conversation with the *mafioso* mayor, then indicated where he thought Serafino to be. Piet returned with one of the houseboys and coffee on a tray round about then. It only took me a couple of minutes to give them a description of the terrain, ending with my own solution to the problem.

Legrande looked glum. Having served with a colonial parachute regiment in Indo-China and, later, Algeria, he'd as much experience of that kind of thing as Burke and probably more.

"I don't like it," he said. "A night drop into country like that is asking for it. All we need is for one of us to break a leg and we're in real trouble."

"It's the only way," I said. "Otherwise we might as well pack our bags and go home."

"Stacey's right," Burke said briskly. "We've no choice. Now, let's get down to the details."

I stood up. "You'll have to manage without me. I'm going out."

He looked at me with a frown. "Don't be absurd. We've got to get this thing organised."

"That's your job. You're supposed to be in charge. I spent a long, hot afternoon sorting the situation out for you while you lay flat on your back tanked up to the ears."

I found myself leaning on the table, caught in our first public confrontation. It was as if Piet and Legrande weren't there—as if we were quite alone. There was a slight puzzled frown on his face, something close to pain in his eyes.

He wanted to ask me why, I knew that. Instead, he said quietly, "All right, Stacey, if that's the way you want it."

He went back to examining the map and I straightened.

Legrande looked completely mystified, but Piet's face was white and angry. I ignored them both and went out.

I showered, then pulled on my old bathrobe and went back into the bedroom, towelling my hair. At that precise moment, the door opened and Piet Jaeger came in.

He slammed it shut and glared at me. "What in the hell are you playing at? You shamed him in front of all of us, the man who's done more for you than anyone else in the world."

"I'll tell you what he did for me," I said. "He taught me three things. To shoot my enemy from cover instead of face-to-face, to kill, not to wound, and that a bullet in the back is to be preferred to one from the front. Quite an education. Oh, there have been one or two other items in between, but those are the salient features."

"You owe him everything." Piet was almost beside himself. "He saved you twice. We said no walking wounded at Lagona, but when the chips were down and you got it in the leg, what did he do?"

"So he made them carry me out. I'd love to know why."

"You rotten bastard." His South African accent had noticeably thickened. "He's worth three of you any day of the week. You aren't fit to walk in his shadow."

In a way I was sorry for him. I suppose a lot of his anger came down to plain jealousy. He loved Burke, I realised that now, and had probably always suffered me in silence. I had been with Burke from the beginning and he was right—by all the rules I should have been given a bullet in the head, the mercenary law to save me from falling into the hands of the simbas alive. But Burke had ordered them to carry me out. For Piet that must have been about as easy to take as a lump of glass in the gut.

"Go on, get out of it," I said. "Go and smooth his wrinkled brow or whatever you do together in the night watches."

He swung hard, the kind of punch that would have knocked my head from my shoulders had it landed. I made sure it didn't, allowing myself to roll backwards across the bed. I didn't fancy my chances in any kind of a fair fight. He hadn't been in jail lately so he was fitter than I was and had a twenty-five pound advantage in weight.

He scrambled across the bed, trying to get at me, got caught up in the sheets and fell on his face. I kicked him in the head, which didn't accomplish much as I was barefooted, but it shook him for a moment and by the time he was on his feet I had the Smith & Wesson in my hand.

"By God, I'll have you now, Wyatt."

He plunged forward and I shot the lobe off his left ear. He screamed like a woman and his hand went to the side of his head as blood spurted. He stared at me in horror and then the door burst open and Legrande appeared. A second later, he was pulled out of the way and Burke entered, the Browning in his hand.

He got between us fast, I'll say that for him. "For God's sake, what's going on here?"

"You'd better get your bloody lover boy out of it if you want to keep him in one piece," I said. "This time I only nicked him. I'd be just as happy to make it two in the belly and he can take his own sweet time about dying."

A good ninety per cent of my anger was simulated and I even allowed my gun hand to shake a little. The total effect on Burke was remarkable. The skin tightened across the cheekbones, something stirred in his eyes and, for a moment, hate looked out at me. I think it was then, at that precise moment, that I knew we were finally finished. That whatever had been between us was dust and ashes.

He allowed the Browning to drop to his side, turned and took Piet by the arm. "Better let me have a look at that for you."

They left without a word. Legrande hesitated and said slowly, "Look, Stacey, maybe we should have words."

I'd never seen him look so troubled. "Go on, get out of it," I said. "I'm sick to death of the lot of you."

I gave him a shove into the corridor and slammed the door. I had a hard job keeping my laughter down. *So now it was Stacey the wild man?* Let them sort that out.

It was only later, alone in the silence, that I discovered that my hand really had begun to shake. I threw the Smith & Wesson onto the bed and dressed quickly.

I'd hung on to the keys of the Fiat and when I went down to the courtyard it was still there. As I climbed behind the wheel Legrande arrived and opened the other door.

"I've got to talk to you, Stacey. I don't know which way I'm pointing."

I shook my head. "You wouldn't be welcome where I'm going."

"As far as the village then. There's a cafe there. We could have a drink."

"Suit yourself, but I can't give you long."

He scrambled in and I drove away. He lit one of his eternal Gauloises and sat back, an expression of settled gloom on his hard, peasant face. He looked more like a Basque than anything else, which wasn't surprising as he came from a village just over the border from Andorra.

He was a close man, one of the most efficient killers I have ever known, but not, I think, by instinct. He was not a cruel man by nature and I had seen him carry a child through twenty miles of the worst country in the Congo rather than leave it to die. He was a product of his times more than anything. A member of the Resistance during the war, he had killed his first man at the age of fourteen. Later had come the years of bloody conflict in the swamps of Indo-China, the humiliation of Dien Bien Phu followed by a Viet prison camp.

Men like him who had been through the fire swore that

it would never happen again. They read Mao Tse-tung on guerrilla warfare and went to Algeria and fought the same kind of war against the same faceless enemy, fighting fire with fire, only to find at the end a greater humiliation than ever. Legrande had come down on the side of the OAS and had fled to the Congo from yet another defeat.

I wondered sometimes what he lived for and sitting in the small cafe in the candlelight he looked old and used up as if he had done everything there was to do.

He swallowed the brandy he had ordered and called for another. "What's wrong between you and the Colonel, Stacey?"

"You tell me."

He shook his head. "He's changed—just in this last six months he's changed. God knows why, but something's eating him, that's for sure."

"I can't help you," I said. "I'm as much in the dark as you are. Maybe Piet can tell you. They seem thick enough."

He was surprised. "That's been going on for years now, ever since the Kasai. I thought you knew."

I smiled. "I only believed in story-book heroes until recently. How long has he been drinking?"

"It came with the general change and he goes at it privately, too. I don't like that. Do you think he's up to this thing?"

"We won't know that till it happens." I finished my brandy and got up. "Must go now, Jules. Can you get back all right?"

He nodded and looked up at me, a strange expression on his face. "Maybe he's like me, Stacey, maybe he's just survived too long. Sometimes I feel I've no right to be here at all, can you understand that? If you think that way for long enough, you lose all sense of reality."

His words haunted me as I went out to the Fiat and drove away.

The Bechstein sounded as good as ever as I waited for my grandfather to appear. I tried a little Debussy and the first of the three short movements of Ravel's *Sonatina*. After that I got ambitious, sorted out some music and worked my way through Bach's *Prelude and Fugue in E flat minor*. Lovely, ice-cold stuff that still sounded marvellous, even if my technique had dulled a little over the years.

When I finished, there was still no sign of him. I went looking and was surprised to find him sitting on the terrace with a bottle and a couple of glasses in front of him.

"I didn't want to disturb you," he said. "I've been listening from here. It sounded fine."

"At a distance."

He smiled and filled a glass for me. It was Marsala and very good. Not one of my favourites, but I couldn't have said so had my life depended on it because suddenly and for no apparent reason there was an intimacy between us. Something very real, something I didn't want to lose.

"How did you get on in the mountains?" he asked me.

"Didn't Marco give you a report? Hasn't he returned yet?"

He managed an expression of vague bewilderment which didn't impress me in the slightest. "Marco has been in Palermo all day as he is every Friday. It's the biggest day of the week for us. Receipts to check, the bank to see. You know how it is in business."

I smiled. "All right, we'll play the game your way. I saw Cerda, who told me where he thinks Serafino may be found. Catching him there is another matter with a shepherd whistling from every crag, but it could be done."

"Is it permitted to ask how?"

I told him and he frowned slightly. "You've done this sort of thing before?"

"Oh, yes, I'm quite the commando."

"But to jump into darkness in country like that sounds a more than usually dangerous practise."

"Possibly, but it can be done."

"Why, Stacey? Why do you want to do this thing? Why do you live this way?"

"There's always the money."

He shook his head. "We've been into that—not good enough. No, when I look at you I see myself forty years ago. *Mafioso* branded clean to the bone."

"Which is another way of saying I like to play the game," I said, "and a savage, bloody little game it is, but it's all I've got. That and Burke."

I stood up and moved to the edge of the terrace and he said softly, "You don't like him?"

"It goes deeper than that. Everything I am, he made. People keep telling me that and I'm tired of hearing it." I turned to face him. "He taught me that if you're going to kill it may as well be from the back as the front, that there's no difference. But he's wrong."

I desperately wanted him to understand, more than I had ever wanted anything. He sat there looking at me gravely. "Without the rules, it's nothing—no sense to any of it. With them, there's still something to hang on to."

He nodded, a slight smile on his face. "Something else you brought out of this Hole of yours, Stacey?"

"I suppose so."

"Then it was worth it." He took out a cigar. "Now go back to the piano like a good boy and play me your mother's favourite piece again."

The music was absolute perfection and brought her back to me like a living presence. All the sadness of life, all its beauty, caught in an exquisite moment that seemed to go on forever. When I finished, there were tears on my face.

When I got back, Hoffer had returned and there was

some sort of council of war going on in the lounge. Burke looked completely different. He'd shaved and wore a khaki shirt with epaulets which gave him a certain military air.

But the change went deeper. There was a briskness about him, an authority I had not seen since my return. When I went in, he glanced up from the map and said calmly, "Ah, there you are, Stacey. I've just been going over things with Mr. Hoffer."

Piet stood in the background, a wad of sticking plaster moulding his right ear, Legrande beside him. The South African simply didn't look at me as I went to the table.

"This is one hell of a good idea," Hoffer said, rubbing his hands together. "Colonel Burke tells me it's primarily your suggestion."

Burke's voice was flat and colourless as he cut in. "The trouble is getting to Serafino before he realises we're in the area. His camp, as we understand it, is about four thousand five hundred feet up on the eastern slopes of the mountain. The idea is that we make a night drop onto a plateau about a thousand feet below the summit on the western side."

"Then you cross over and catch him with his pants down?"

Hoffer's choice of phrase was unfortunate under the circumstances, but Burke nodded. "We should get over the summit at least by dawn. On the other side there's a forest belt about a thousand feet down. Oak, birch, some pine, I understand. Once we reach that we'll have plenty of cover on the final stretch."

Hoffer seemed genuinely excited as he examined the map. "You know something? For the first time I really believe there's a chance. Let's all have a drink on it."

"Another time if you don't mind," I said. "I could do with an early night. It's been a long day."

He was pleasant enough about it and, as no one pressed

me to stay, I left them and went up to my room. Not that I could sleep when I did go to bed. I lay there with the french windows open because of the heat and after a while it started to shower. It was round about that time that Rosa arrived.

She took off the silk kimono she was wearing. "Look, no trouser suit."

When she got in beside me, she was shivering, though from desire or cold was uncertain and whether she was there for herself or Hoffer didn't really seem to matter. It was nice, lying there in the darkness holding her in the hollow of my arm, listening to the rain, even when she fell asleep on me!

10

AS I FOUND out later, Burke didn't go to bed. Instead, he flew to Crete in the Cessna to pick up a few things we were going to need and was back just before eleven on Saturday morning.

Sunday, being the conventional day of rest, seemed as reasonable a time to catch Serafino napping as we were likely to find, which meant going in that night. There was almost a full moon, which didn't please Burke much, but he was impatient to be off now that the ball was rolling again and bustled around, full of energy, checking everything.

We used a small private airstrip not far from the villa, a cow pasture really, with a hangar that was barely large enough to get the Cessna inside.

The plane was the 401 model with eight seats and we had those out for a start. A particularly good point was the Airstair door amidships which would give us a clear exit, something we badly needed if all four of us were to get out in time to drop in a nice tight group.

The pilot, a man called Nino Verda, was ex-Italian Airforce, about thirty from the look of him and, according to Hoffer, the best money could buy. He needed to be. To fly that kind of country in the dark, graze a six-thousand-foot mountain and give us an eight-hundred-foot drop over that plateau was going to take genius.

We were using the X-type parachute, the kind British paratroopers used before they changed to the new NATO one. Burke preferred the X-type. It got you down faster and could be guided with greater accuracy. The reserve chutes were of the same type and identical with those we had used in the Congo.

Our weapons were unconventional by some standards, but proved in combat, the only realistic test. We were using the Chinese AK assault rifle, probably the most reliable automatic combat rifle in the world at that time and the new Israeli submachine gun, the Uzi, which was better than the Sterling in every way.

Two grenades each, a commando knife—the list seemed endless. Burke even had a kit inspection with each man's camouflaged jump suit laid out together with every item of equipment.

And he went over the operation with the map and a stopwatch so many times that even Piet Jaeger looked sick by late evening. Towards me he seemed no different and I suppose any touch of formality in our relationship could have been put down to the exigencies of the situation.

At dinner, Hoffer was joviality personified. Only the best was good enough although Burke put his foot down as regards alcohol. But the food was excellent. Surprisingly, I found an appetite for it and Rosa was there, wearing her best, looking absolutely magnificent.

Afterwards, Burke took us through the plan again in detail, including the walk-out if everything went well, which he estimated would take eight or nine hours to the point on the Bellona road where we were to be met by Hoffer himself with the necessary transport.

He shook hands with us all solemnly when Burke had

finished and made a little speech about how much he appreciated what we were doing and how he hoped before long to have his stepdaughter with him again, God willing, which I thought was pushing it a bit far.

Later, when I was changing in my room, Rosa appeared. She zipped up the front of my camouflaged suit and kissed me on the cheek. "From you or from Hoffer?" I said.

"From me." She touched my face briefly. "Come back safe."

She hesitated in the doorway, and looked at me, a strange expression on her face. She wanted to speak, wanted like hell to tell me something and was desperately afraid of the consequences.

I felt a sudden rush of affection for her, shook my head and smiled. "Don't say it, Rosa, not if you're truly afraid of him."

"But I am," she said, her face white. "He can be cruel, oh, so cruel, Stacey. You couldn't imagine."

"Tell me about it when I return, when it doesn't matter any more." I opened the door and kissed her as a woman should be kissed, moulding her ripeness into me. "I survive all things, Rosa Solazzo, especially the Hoffers of this world."

After she had gone, I buckled on my belt with the Smith & Wesson in its spring holster and adjusted my beret. The man who stared out at me from the mirror was a stranger, someone from before the Hole. What then was he doing here? It was quite a thought, but the wrong time to be asking questions like that, and I left and went down to join the others.

The cruising speed of a Cessna 401 is up to 261 miles per hour, which meant that we could expect to be over the target in twenty minutes. We delayed take-off for an hour because the night was still too bright for Burke's liking,

but the overcast promised by the met forecast didn't ma-
terialise and he reluctantly gave the word to go at 1 A.M.

Verda had logged an internal flight to Gela with the
authorities at Punta Raisi, just in case questions were
asked, which meant flying through the great divide anyway. A minor divergence would take him into the area of
the drop and within minutes he could be back on course
again.

Including the training Burke had given us in the Congo,
I had jumped nine times in all, so this would make ten—a
nice round number. I had never particularly enjoyed the
experience. A paratrooper is a clumsy creature, hampered
by the requirements of his calling. The X-type parachute
weighs twenty-eight pounds and the reserve chute around
twenty-four. A fair weight to start with. Add to that a supply bag carrying anything up to a hundred pounds and it's
hardly surprising that the only movement possible is down-
wards.

Even removing the passenger seats from the interior
gave us barely enough room to manoeuvre with all that
equipment. Burke had rigged a static line of his own devising and he and Verda had carefully removed the Airstair door, which was fine as long as no one fell out before
we got there.

A lot of things were going through my head as I squatted
on the floor in line as the Cessna lifted smoothly into the
air. The die was cast now, we were on our way—no
turning back and I still wasn't certain about anything, except that everyone in sight seemed to be lying to me, including Rosa.

For some unaccountable reason that one hurt and when
I analysed my feelings I realised with a shock that I had
liked her. Really liked her. She had guts and her own
special brand of integrity and I knew beyond a shadow of
a doubt that her final appearance in my room had been
completely personal. She had come to say goodbye be-

cause she wanted to and not because Hoffer or anyone else had pressured her.

We were flying at eight thousand feet now and the view was certainly spectacular. Chains of mountains, peaks and ridges, white in the moonlight, the valleys between dark with shadow.

The journey passed completely without incident and was so short that it was something of a shock when the red light Verda had rigged blinked rapidly several times. When I looked out of the window I could see the jagged peak of Monte Cammarata, the western slope and then, as we slanted down, the dark, saucershaped plateau which was the dropping zone, the waterfall next to it bright in the moonlight, a clear marker.

Verda swung into the wind and turned, coming in so close to the rocky precipice that lifted to the summit above the plateau that the heart moved inside me. We got a brief idea of what it was going to be like and then he swung the Cessna into the void.

As he turned to come in again, Burke who was the lead man, stood up and slipped onto the static line. Piet followed suit, then Legrande and I brought up the rear. My stomach was hollow, mouth dry, and I shuffled forward with the others, caught in a nightmare of suspense.

The red light blinked once, then twice; the Cessna rocked in some kind of turbulence and Burke went out through the door. Piet must have been right on top of him, Legrande hard on his heels.

And then it was my turn. The wind howled past the gaping doorway. Only a madman could venture out there, I told myself and fell head-first, somersaulting.

I released the supply bag I had been clutching tightly in my arms and it fell to swing twenty feet below on the end of a line clipped to my waist. And I was swinging too, beneath the dark khaki umbrella, the most beautiful sight in the world at that moment.

When you jump at eight hundred feet, it takes exactly thirty seconds to hit the deck, which doesn't give you long to sort yourself out. That close to the rock face, there were down-drafts and I started to oscillate. As usual, once you were out in the open, the light didn't seem anything like as good. I caught a brief glimpse of one chute then another like dark thistledown, drifting into the shadows beside the waterfall, and then I was moving in fast myself.

The trouble with a night-drop is that usually you can't see the ground, which accounts for the high proportion of broken limbs on that type of operation, people being caught by surprise and landing too stiffly.

That was one thing I liked about the supply bag dangling down there at the end of a twenty-foot line. Unless you are oscillating alarmingly, the bag hits the deck first with a solid thump, warning you to get ready.

I just made it in time. The supply bag thudded into the ground and I followed a split second later, rolling into a patch of surprisingly springy turf. I rolled again and came to rest, a shoulder of rock nudging me in the ribs.

I lay there, winded, and someone came close and leaned over me. There was the gleam of steel and I got my hand up just in time, the Smith & Wesson ready.

"I was only going to cut your line," Piet Jaeger said.

"Are you sure it wasn't my throat you were aiming for?"

"Another time," he said. "When you aren't so useful. When we don't need you any more."

He sounded as if he meant it and sliced through my belt line and pulled my supply bag clear. I struggled out of my harness and got rid of the chute. Now that I was down, the light seemed much better and I could see Burke and Legrande approaching carrying their chutes and supply bags. The Frenchman was limping, but it turned out to be nothing serious. In his case, his oscillation had been so great that he had hit the ground before his supply bag, when unprepared. He'd obviously had a bad shaking, but he made light of it as we unpacked.

The supply bags held the Commando rucksacks containing food and water, our weapons and extra ammunition, and, when they were empty, went into a convenient crevasse together with the parachutes.

We squatted in the shelter of the rocks and Burke passed round a flask of brandy. I took a long pull and found myself smiling, grateful to be alive, two feet on solid earth again as the warmth spread through me.

"There's no point in hanging about," he said. "Straight up to the top from here. We've got to get over and into those trees while it's still dark."

Which didn't give us long because dawn was officially at ten past four and we moved out at once in single file. I took the lead because in theory, at least, I knew more about the terrain than anyone else and followed a route which took us straight up the side of the waterfall.

It was a marvellous night, the moon almost full, a trace or two of cloud around, stars glittering everywhere. The mountains marched into the distance, ridge after ridge of them, and far to the east moonlight glittered on Etna's snowy peak.

The valleys were dark, but four thousand feet below and a couple of miles to the right in the general direction of Bellona a single light gleamed. I wondered if it could be Cerda sitting up and wondering how we were making out, for nothing was more certain than that my grandfather would have kept him fully informed.

A good actor, Cerda, one had to admit that. Even the gun behind his back had all been part of the show. He had behaved in a way it was reasonable to suppose I would expect him to—very clever. His one flaw had been his apparent ignorance of the presence of Joanna Truscott in the mountains. Hardly likely in a man who knew everything else there was to know about Serafino.

Still, an excellent performance with Marco keeping out of the way in the back room. You really couldn't trust anyone in this affair, or so it seemed to me then.

It was just after three when we made the summit and I dropped into a hollow between rocks and waited for the others. I was tired and I suppose the truth was that I wasn't really fit enough for this kind of game yet. On the other hand, the others didn't look too good either, Legrande particularly, and Burke seemed to be having difficulty with his breathing.

He passed the brandy round again, probably as an excuse to have one himself. "So far so good. We've got just under an hour to get down a thousand feet or so. If we can do that I think we'll have it made."

He nodded to me. "All right, Stacey."

So I was still leading the way. I stood up and moved out, more conscious than ever that he was at the back of me.

It wasn't easy going at all. The ground was rough and treacherous and, with the moon almost down, the light on that side of the mountain was very bad indeed. In places there were great aprons of shale that were as treacherous underfoot as ice, sliding like water at the slightest movement.

I paused after half an hour on a small plateau and waited for them. In the east there was already a perceptible lightening of the sky on the rim of the world and I knew we were not going to make it unless the going changed completely.

Piet arrived first, seemingly in excellent shape, and then Legrande, who slumped to the ground and looked pretty tired to me. Burke brought up the rear and I noticed again that his breathing wasn't good.

"What have we stopped for?" he demanded.

I shrugged. "I thought we could all do with a breather."

"To hell with that. We'll never make it at this rate."

He sounded good and angry and I cut him off with a quick gesture. "Okay—you're the boss."

I started down again, pushing myself hard, taking a chance or two on occasion, at one point sliding a good hundred feet on a great wave of shale that seemed as if it would never stop moving. Not that it did any good. In the grey light of dawn, we were still three hundred feet up from the first scattering of trees.

I've never felt so naked in my life as when I led the way down that final stretch of bare hillside. It was exactly twenty minutes to five when I reached the outer belt of trees.

11

AS THE greyness spread among the trees, we crouched in a circle and had something to eat. Burke seemed fine when sitting down and his breathing was normal again. But Legrande looked his age and more; the lines on his face were deeply etched. He was getting old, that was the trouble; too old for this sort of caper.

Even Piet looked tired and cold crouched there with the mist curling from the damp ground. The heavy brigade, that's what we'd always called Legrande and him. There had been occasions when the sight of those two arriving shoulder to shoulder, smashing their way through with the force of a runaway train, had been enough to make you stand up and cheer, but not any more. Times changed and people changed with them—that was life and the pattern of things.

I shivered slightly. I did not like this kind of grey dawning. It reminded me of too many similar ones and a lot of good men gone. I lit a cigarette which tasted foul, but I persisted and Burke moved over and unfolded his copy of the map.

"We can't be more than five hundred feet above this

shepherd's hut where he's supposed to be hanging out. It might be an idea if you made a quick reconnaissance. We'll wait here. I'll give you three-quarters of an hour." He added in a low voice, "I think Legrande could do with the rest. He looks shot to me."

I got to my feet. "I think you've got a point there. I'll see you later."

I moved down through the trees. On the rockier slopes they were cork-oak and holly-oak, but then I entered a belt of beech and pine and the going became a lot easier.

A fox broke cover, giving me so much of a fright that I almost ended his days for him, which would have been fatal for all of us, but there was plenty of wildlife on the mountain besides Serafino and his boys. Wildcats and martens and the odd wolf, although they all tended to run the opposite way at the first smell of a man.

I made good progress now and broke into a trot, my rifle at the trail, sliding down the occasional slope on my backside, and within fifteen minutes of leaving the others I had descended a good three hundred feet.

There was a freshwater stream over on my right. I worked my way across, lay on my belly and splashed water on my face. It seemed as good a route down as any and it was more than likely that any shepherd building a hut would place it as close to water as possible, especially when you considered what it was like in this country during the summer.

It was the voice I heard first, a kind of smothered gasp that was cut off sharply. I paused, dropping to one knee. There was silence, then a vigorous splashing and another sharp cry.

I had seen the Honourable Joanna Truscott twice in my life, both times on photos which Hoffer had shown us. In one she had been dressed for skiing, in the other, for a garden party at Buckingham Palace. It was difficult to accept that the girl I watched now from the bushes, floundering naked in a hollow among the trees where the stream had formed a small pool, was the same.

Her hair was tied back into a kind of eighteenth-century queue and her face, neck and arms were gypsy-brown from the sun. The rest of her was milk white and boyish, the breasts almost non-existent, although the hips could only have belonged to a woman.

She scrambled out and rubbed herself down with an old blanket. I didn't bother looking away. For one thing she didn't know I was there and for another there was something rather sexless about her. Strange how some women can set one aflame with all the fury of a petrol-soaked bonfire in an instant and others have no effect whatsoever.

She pulled on a pair of old trousers that had definitely seen better days, a man's shirt, green woollen sweater with holes in the elbows, and bound a red scarf around her head, knotting it under her chin.

As she sat down to pull on a pair of Spanish felt boots, I stepped out of the trees and said cheerfully, "Good morning."

She was a tough one all right. "And good morning to you," she replied calmly and started to get up.

"No need to be alarmed," I said rather unnecessarily. "My name is Wyatt—Stacey Wyatt. I'm from your stepfather, Karl Hoffer. I've three friends waiting for me now up the mountain. We've come to get you out."

God, what a fool I was. She was on her own and unguarded, obviously free to roam at will. Why on earth that didn't strike me at once, I'll never know. It had been a strenuous night—perhaps I was tired.

"What am I expected to do—stand up and cheer?" she said coolly in that beautifully clipped, upper-crust English voice. "How did he tell you to dispose of me? Gun, knife or blunt instrument?"

I stared at her in astonishment and at the same time some kind of light started to dawn. She had turned away from me slightly. When I got the front view again, she was holding an old Beretta automatic pistol in her right hand and looked as if she knew exactly what to do with it.

"Would you mind going into rather more detail," I told her. "I'm afraid I'm not with you."

"Why don't you pull the other one," she suggested crisply.

I was still holding the AK at the trail. I dropped it at my feet and put the Uzi beside it. "Look, no hands."

She wasn't impressed. "What about the thing in the holster?"

I removed the Smith & Wesson, laid it down, then walked back three paces, squatted against a holly-oak and took out my cigarettes.

"Like one?"

She shook her head. "I want to live to a ripe old age."

"If you think it's worth it." I lit one myself. "Now I'm going to talk and you're going to listen and then you can shoot me—if you still want to."

"We'll see," she said calmly. "Only make it quick. I haven't had any breakfast."

So I told her in a few brief sentences and when I was finished her expression hadn't altered in the slightest. "Let me get this straight. My stepfather told you I was abducted by Serafino Lentini and held to ransom. That he paid up, but that Serafino decided to have his own wicked way with me after all and kept the money into the bargain."

"That's about the size of it."

"A lie, Mr. Wyatt, from beginning to end."

"I thought so."

She showed her surprise. "I don't understand."

"I happen to know that because of injuries sustained under police interrogation some years ago, Serafino Lentini isn't physically capable of taking that kind of interest in any woman."

"But if you knew that, if you realised there was something phoney about my stepfather's story from the beginning, why did you come?"

"I've always been insatiably curious." I grinned. "The money was good and he made you sound rather interesting. Tell me, did you really sleep with the chauffeur when you were fourteen?"

Her eyes widened, she gasped and what I can only describe as a virginal flush tinged her cheeks.

"Sorry," I said. "It's obvious now that he has an unusually inventive streak."

"You want the facts? I'll give them to you." She wasn't pointing the Beretta at me any longer and she looked mad. "As they say about life insurance, I'm worth more dead than alive. My mother left me everything in trust with my stepfather as executor. Something of a mistake on her part. I'm twenty-one in another three weeks and get personal control of the whole thing. If I die before then Hoffer gets the lot. Two and a half million."

It certainly made what he was paying us sound very marginal indeed.

"The only true thing he appears to have told you," she went on, "is the fact that he gave Serafino Lentini twenty-five thousand dollars, but for a different reason. I was to be ambushed when driving alone to visit friends at Villalba one evening, robbed and shot dead beside my car, where I would be easily found and identified, apparently just another victim of a bandit outrage."

"But Serafino wouldn't play?"

"He intended to at first. Standing there beside my car that evening after he and his men had stopped me. I thought my last hour had come. I don't think I'll ever be as close to death again."

"What made him change his mind?"

"He's told me since that he liked the look of me. That I reminded him of his younger sister who died in childbirth a year ago. I think the real truth is that he doesn't like my stepfather. It seems they had dealings before, although he's never told me much about that."

"Then why did he do business with Hoffer at all?"

"He wanted money—big money. He's enthusiastic about only one thing—the idea of emigrating to South America and leaving this life behind. I think I'm alive because it suddenly struck him that it would be rather amusing to take Hoffer's money and not carry out his side of the bargain."

"So he whisked you off to the mountains?"

"I've been with him ever since."

"Doesn't it ever worry you that he might change his mind on another whim?"

She shook her head. "Not in the slightest. Since I explained the real facts of the situation he and his men are only too well aware which side their bread is buttered on."

"But of course," I said softly. "All they've got to do is keep you alive long enough and you'll have all the money in the world."

"Exactly. Once things are settled satisfactorily, I've promised to get them out to South America with a quarter of a million dollars to split between the four of them."

So now all was revealed. *Or was it?* A great deal that had puzzled me was now explained, but there were several things which still didn't make any kind of sense.

She voiced one of them for me. "One thing I can't understand. What were you supposed to do once you got your hands on me?"

"Take you to Hoffer. He's meeting us himself on the Bellona road."

"Didn't he expect me to say anything to you? Weren't you supposed to notice when you got here that I wasn't the slave of Serafino's passion that he made out?"

Which had been worrying me for some time and yet I could think of no possible explanation except for the one she offered me herself a moment later.

"Which takes us back to square one," she said. "The only logical explanation. That you dropped in to finish me off along with Serafino and his men. Then my stepfather goes to the police, wringing his hands, giving them some story about how he's been afraid for my life and didn't dare seek official help before, but now he can't go on. The police make an official search and find what's left of us."

"Wouldn't they want to know who was responsible?"

"There are several groups in the mountains, just like Serafino and his men, and there's no love lost." She shrugged. "It would be reasonable to suppose that one of them was responsible. All very sad, but nice and tidy for my stepfather. When you think of it, it is the only explanation that makes any kind of sense."

Her hand started to bring up the Beretta again. It was her eyes that warned me and the sudden, pinched look about the mouth, not that I was particularly alarmed.

I came up in an unnecessarily spectacular spring, got my shoulder to her knees and had her on her back in a moment. Once on top, the war was over, although a certain amount of wriggling continued until I clamped a knee across each of her arms.

I held up the Beretta and slipped the safety catch. "It just won't fire until you do that. Try again."

I dropped it on her chest, got up and turned my back on her. I lit another cigarette, an ostentatious bit of theatricality, and when I turned again she was standing staring at me in bewilderment, the Beretta swinging loosely from one hand and pointing directly into the ground.

"But it still doesn't make sense," she said.

She was right—it didn't. The only thing which filled her true circumstances was that we had been sent to kill her and we had not.

Or had we . . . ?

It was suddenly cold and my throat went dry. No, it wasn't possible and I tried to push the thought away from me. Burke would never have stood still for a thing like that.

In any case, I wasn't allowed to take it any further. Someone jumped on my back, an arm clamped around my throat, and down I went.

Someone once said that God made some men big and some small and left it to Colonel Colt to even things up. As a philosophy where violence is concerned, it's always appealed to me and like most relatively small men I've never been much good at the hand-to-hand stuff.

The arm about my throat was doing a nice, efficient job of cutting off the air supply. I was choking, there was a roaring in my ears. Somewhere the girl was shouting and then he made the mistake of moving position and I managed an elbow strike to his privates.

It was only half on target and there wasn't much zip behind it, but it was enough. I was released with a curse, rolled over twice and fetched up against a holly-oak tree.

Not that it did me much good. My head went back with a crack and the muzzle of a rifle was shoved into the side of my neck.

12

THE M-1 .30-calibre is the semi-automatic rifle that got most American infantrymen through the Second World War, which meant that the one which was about to blow a hole in me now had been around for quite a while. On the other hand, it had obviously been cared for like a lover. The stock was polished, the gunmetal shone with oil and the whole thing looked as lethal as anyone could wish, just like the man who was holding it, Serafino Lentini.

"Serafino, stop!" the girl shouted in Italian. "You mustn't shoot him—you mustn't!"

He was wearing an old corduroy suit, leather leggings to his knees, and the face beneath the cloth cap was recklessly handsome in spite of the week-old stubble of beard and the dirty black patch over the right eye. A gay lad, this, a bravo straight out of the sixteenth century. I could almost see him in doublet and hose. A kiss for a woman, a blow for a man. I smiled, remembering the old joke. Very funny, except that with this boy you'd probably get a knife in the gut if you got in his way.

The two men behind him were just a blur; it was his

face that loomed large for me in all the world at that moment. He grinned wolfishly and pushed off the safety.

"Careful," I said. "Cursed is the man who spills the blood of his own."

The old Sicilian proverb had about the same effect as a good stiff hook to the chin. His eye, that one good eye of his, seemed to widen, but most important of all, the barrel of the M-1 was removed from my neck.

"Quick," he said. "Who are you?"

"Barbaccia's grandson. We're kin through my grandmother's family."

"Mother of God, but I remember you as a boy." The safety catch clicked on again, the most reassuring thing to happen for some time. "Once when I was fourteen, my old man went to see the *capo* on family business. I had to wait at the gate. I saw you walking in the garden playing with a dog. All white with black spots. I forget what they call them."

"Dalmatians," I said and remembered old Trudi for the first time in years.

"The *capo's* American grandson in his pretty clothes. God, how I hated you that day. I wanted to rub mud in your hair." He produced a stub of cigar from one pocket, lit it and squatted in front of me. "I heard you and the *capo* didn't get on after they got your mother that way." He spat. "Mafia pigs. Still, from what I hear, he's almost swept the board clean."

I wanted to ask him what he meant, but the occasion didn't seem appropriate. He reached over and fingered my jump suit.

"What's all this? When I first saw you through the trees I thought they'd brought the troops in again."

By now I had everything in focus including the girl and the two specimens who were examining the assault rifle with interest. They were in the same unshaven condition as Serafino, the same ragged state. Each of them had a shotgun slung from the shoulder.

I sat up wearily. "I can't go through all that again. Ask her."

He didn't argue, simply turned and went to Joanna Truscott. They moved away a little, talking in low tones, and I got my cigarettes out. As I lit one, the man who was taking a sight along the barrel of the AK, lowered it and snapped a finger.

I tossed the packet across. There was a definite physical resemblance between them and I said, "You're the Vivaldi boys, I suppose."

The one with the rifle nodded. "That's right. I'm August—he's Pietro. Don't expect much from him, though." He tapped his head. "He had his difficulties and he can't speak."

Pietro did a semblance of a jig and his mouth opened, exposing half-a-dozen black stubs and nothing else. He had a great foolish grin that reminded me strongly of the Cheshire cat. I suppose he had exactly the same smile on his face as he blew someone's head off.

In fact the head might very well be mine, which was a cheering thought, and then Serafino came back and I could tell from the look on his face that everything was going to be all right.

"It's ironic," he said, "when I remember how often old Barbaccia has tried to have me put down. But then, we are not of the blood."

A nice distinction, but sufficient.

"Can I have my weapons back?" I asked.

"I don't know about that, we could do with them ourselves." He was obviously unwilling, but decided to make a gesture. "Give him the pop-gun back. Hang on to the others."

August handed me the Smith & Wesson, looking more than happy, and I pushed it into the spring holster. Had they only known it, at that range I could have given each of them a bullet in the head within the second.

We went down through the trees in a line, Serafino and I together at the rear. Apparently he still had Hoffer's twenty-five thousand buried in an old biscuit tin somewhere in the area. He thought the whole thing very funny and laughed frequently in the telling.

"So, I've killed a few people in my time. That's life." He scratched his face vigorously. "I did a couple of jobs for Hoffer when he was having trouble with construction workers on the new road through the mountains. Leaned on one or two and then we dumped some trade unionist down a crevasse. And then he gets in touch with me through a friend and lays out this job concerning the girl."

"Did you know who she was?"

"Not a hint. He told me she was a blackmailer—that she could ruin him unless she had her mouth closed for keeps. I'd insisted on payment in advance so I had the cash anyway and when I saw her, I liked her." He grinned ruefully. "Not that I'm half the man I used to be, so she'd nothing to worry about there."

"Yes, I heard about that."

He laughed uproariously. "Life, it's a bastard, eh? No, I liked her for the way she stuck out her chin and stood up straight when she thought I was going to shoot her. It put me off, her standing there like some princess from Rome. Then it struck me as how funny it might be to put one over on Hoffer, seeing I already had the cash. He's a rat and anyway I don't like Mafia."

He spat again, I stumbled, put off my stroke to such an extent that I almost lost my balance. I grabbed him by the arm. "Hoffer is Mafia?"

"Didn't you know? One of those American syndicate boys the Yanks deported during the last few years."

And my grandfather hadn't said a word. "Does the girl know?"

"Not really." He shook his head. "Oh, she thinks he's a swine all right, but this is only her second visit to Sicily. To her Mafia is the two lines in the tourist handbook that says it's a romantic memory."

Which was reasonable enough. What would she know, spending the greater part of the year at some fancy English boarding school and most of the rest following the social round in France, Switzerland and the usual places. We had something in common there.

"So Hoffer is working for the Society over here?"

"Do me a favour." Serafino seemed surprised. "You know the rule. Once in, never out. He's the last of half a dozen similar."

"What happened to the others?"

"Two pressed the starters in their Alfas and went straight to hell. The rest were ventilated in one way or another, as I remember. They had the knife out for Barbaccia, but they made a big mistake. The old wolf was a match for all of them."

"The attempt on his life," I said. "The bomb which killed my mother, who was responsible for that?"

"Who knows?" He shrugged. "Any one of them. Does it matter? Barbaccia will have had all of them before he is through."

My flesh crawled at the enormity of it. Vito Barbaccia, Lord of Life and Death. He was well named. I shuddered and went after Serafino, who was striding ahead, whistling cheerfully.

The shepherd's hut looked as if it had been there since time began. It was constructed of rocks and boulders of various sizes, the gaps in between filled with dried mud, and the low roof consisted of sods on top of oak branches. At that point the stream had turned into a brawling torrent, descending rapidly through several deep pools, disappearing over an apron of stone about fifty yards below.

The hut was built into a sloping bank in a clearing beside the stream and looked remarkably homely. A couple of donkeys grazed nearby while three goats and half a dozen chickens moved in and out of the undergrowth, pecking vigorously at the soil.

A boy of eighteen or nineteen, presumably the Joe Ricco whom Cerda had mentioned, crouched over a small fire, feeding the flames beneath a cooking pot with sticks. Except for his youth and red Norman hair, he was depressingly similar in appearance to the rest of them. The same cloth cap, patched suit and leather leggings, the same sullen, brutalised features. He got up, staring at me curiously, and the Vivaldi brothers joined him, crouching to help themselves with a dirty and chipped enamel mug to what vaguely smelt like coffee.

Serafino and Joanna Truscott sat on a log by the stream and he produced from somewhere another piece of cigar and lit it. He looked up into the grey morning. "Still it doesn't make sense." He shook his head. "I'd give a lot to know what Hoffer is playing at."

"Perhaps the whole thing is simpler than we think," Joanna said. "Maybe he assumed you would do anything for money."

"He could be right there," I agreed, but somehow it didn't sound too funny because it sent me off on another train of thought, one I wanted to avoid, but Serafino wouldn't let it alone.

"These friends of yours, you can trust them? They're not making a monkey out of you?"

I thought about it hard and tried to sound confident. "Anything is possible in this life, but I don't think so. There's one way to find out, of course."

"And what is that?"

"I'll go and see them."

He nodded, biting on his cigar, a frown on his face. Joanna Truscott said, "You could make them an offer on my behalf if you like. It would be nice to turn the tables on my stepfather for once." She picked up a stick, snapped it between her hands. "He married my mother for money, did you know that? When she wouldn't give him any more, he got rid of her."

"Are you certain of that?"

She nodded. "Not that I could prove it. He thought he'd get everything because he knew she loved him—loved him to distraction, but he made a mistake. She left me everything, and now he's in trouble—bad trouble."

"What kind?"

"He needs money—a great deal of money. He's frightened, too."

So Mafia was in this after all?

"All right, wait for me here." I looked at my watch, saw that it was an hour since I had left Burke and the others, which meant they would already be on their way down. "I'll be about half an hour."

I thought they might stop me from going, but nobody moved. When I looked back from the edge of the trees, Joanna Truscott had taken off her red scarf and the blond hair gleamed as the first rays of the early morning sun broke through the clouds.

I ploughed up the steep slope, pushing through the undergrowth, and the going was so hard that I had little time to concentrate on anything else except making progress. But I wasn't happy. The trouble was that in my heart I'd never believed Hoffer's story for a moment. Certain aspects of it were always manifestly impossible and if I'd seen the flaws why hadn't Burke?

But then I couldn't believe the second possibility. He'd done many things in his time—aided and abetted by me on occasion. Killed ruthlessly and often without compassion, but as a soldier. It was inconceivable that he would have agreed to murder a young girl for money. In any case, it would not have been possible with the rest of us there.

So deep in thought was I that it was with a sense of surprise that I found myself at the spot by the stream where I had met the Honourable Joanna earlier. I paused to catch my breath and a stick cracked behind me.

"Hold it right there." Piet Jaeger stepped from behind a tree, his assault rifle levelled at my belt.

"Stacey, what happened? We were getting worried."

Burke moved out of the trees with Legrande, and Piet Jaeger went to stand point at the edge of the little clearing automatically. He was a good soldier, always had been, I'll say that for him.

"Well, what happened?" Burke said again. "Did you have any luck?" He frowned suddenly. "Where's your rifle?"

"In custody," I said. "One of Serafino's boys took a fancy to it."

He went very still. "You'd better explain."

I moved to the side of the steam away from Jaeger and Legrande and sat on a boulder. Burke lit a cigarette and squatted before me, his rifle across his knees.

"Okay, what happened? You were supposed to scout, not make contact."

"I found the girl up here on her own having a swim. No guards, no restraint. When I told her who I was from, she expected me to kill her."

"She what?" A look of astonishment appeared on his face.

"As for Serafino and his boys," I went on, "they aren't sweating over her fair white body in turn as Hoffer implied. They're working for her. By staying up here, she stays alive, it's as simple as that."

I gave him the whole story in detail, even the girl's suspicions about her mother's death, and I watched him closely all the time. When I was finished, he got to his feet and stood there, staring down into the water, jiggling a handful of pebbles.

"At least it explains a few things. Hoffer had a word with me just before we left. He said he was worried because the girl had a history of what amounted to a kind of mental instability. That she'd had treatment a couple of times without success. He said she was sex mad and probably enjoying every moment of her experience. He seemed to think she might kick up a fuss about coming with us. He said she very easily became hysterical and was capable of making the wildest accusations." He turned. "You're sure she isn't . . . ?"

I shook my head. "I've spoken to Serafino. He told me he was hired to kill the girl and changed his mind because he wanted to do Hoffer down. He doesn't like him."

"The bastard." Burke threw the pebbles he was holding into the water viciously. "Neither do I."

The main thing which had worried me was now explained and I was conscious of a definite easing of tension and a sudden rush of affection for Burke, coupled with a kind of guilt because I had even admitted the possibility that he was capable of such an act.

He produced his packet of cigarettes for the second time. It was empty and he threw it into the stream. I gave him one of mine and when he lit it I saw that his hands were shaking. He stared out across the water.

"God, what a fool I've been. I knew there was something phoney about the whole thing. From the beginning I knew that, and yet I still let it all happen."

"Why, Sean?" I asked.

"Oh, the money was good and it was the only offer I was likely to get." He shrugged. "You change when you get old, you'll find that out. You grab at straws, take the wrong chances, look the other way when you shouldn't, because all of a sudden, the years are rolling by and you've had it."

He choked suddenly on a mouthful of smoke and doubled over, struggling for breath. While it lasted, it was anything but pleasant. I got an arm around him and he leaned hard on me as he coughed up half his lungs.

After a while, he managed to get his breath and smiled wanly. "Okay now." He slapped his chest. "I'm afraid the old lungs aren't what they used to be."

And in that, there was the answer to many things.

"How bad is it?"

He tried to smile and failed. "Bad enough."

And then he told me. Not, as I was beginning to believe, cancer, but something as bad. Some rare disease in which a fungus-like growth spread like a poisonous weed to choke him. There was no cure and drugs could only halt what was an inevitable decline.

To say that I felt guilty at the general way in which I had misjudged him would be an understatement. I was sick to my stomach. There was no excuse. I should have realised from my knowledge of the man that there had to be some logical explanation for his unlikely behaviour.

I came up with the most banal sentence in the world. "I'm sorry, Sean."

He smiled and slapped me on the shoulder. "Never mind that now, Stacey boy. What's to be done, that's the thing."

I told him about Joanna Truscott's offer. "I don't know what she has in mind, but nobody would lose by it, and I'd like to put one over on Hoffer."

"So would I," he said with some passion. "I'll put it to Piet and Legrande."

They stood together in a huddle, talking, and I realised again how tired Legrande looked as they moved to join me. "That's it then," Burke said. "We've got half our money in advance anyway. Now we'll see if we can make the bastard sweat a little."

He seemed to swallow suddenly and stopped dead, so that for a moment I thought he was having another attack, but nothing could have been further from the truth.

"My God," he said, "we're all forgetting something—something absolutely bloody perfect. Hoffer himself will be waiting with our transport on the Bellona road from noon on."

"You think we could give him a nasty surprise?"

He smiled slightly, that smile of his that was not really a smile at all, looking completely his old self again, a thoroughly dangerous man.

"We can have a damn good try, but we're wasting time talking. We'd better join up with the others as quickly as we can and sort out some sort of plan."

We moved out fast in single file with me in the lead. I felt full of energy, strong enough to take on anything, a weight lifted from my body and brain. As for Burke, however unfortunate his condition, there was relief in it for me as an explanation of the inexplicable change in conduct I had found in him.

I paused on the edge of the clearing, perhaps thirty yards away from the hut. Our approach had obviously been noted and there was no one in sight. I waited for the others to join me and told Burke I would go down alone to pave the way. The brothers Vivaldi and Joe Ricco had looked capable of anything and I didn't want any unfortunate misunderstandings at this stage.

I called out to Serafino as I ploughed down the slope through the undergrowth, hands above my head. When I was half-way across the clearing, the door opened and he peered out cautiously, holding my assault rifle ready.

"It's all right," I said. "Everything is fine."

Joanna Truscott appeared at his shoulder, her face uncertain. "You've managed to persuade them?"

"Better than that. Hoffer's going to show up himself this afternoon on the Bellona road to pick us up. Could be he'll get one hell of a surprise."

I'd spoken in Italian and Serafino's face lit up. "Heh, I like that. I could cut the bastard's throat personally. Okay, Stacey Wyatt, call your friends down."

He whistled sharply and the Vivaldi brothers and Joe Ricco appeared from different places on the edge of the clearing. Serafino grinned apologetically. "I never like to take chances."

I waved Burke and the other two down and the girl moved to my side. "You're certain my stepfather will be there himself?"

"That's what the man said." Burke was half-way down to the clearing now, the others just behind him, and I grinned and gave Joanna Truscott a little push towards him. "Well, here she is, Sean. The purpose of the exercise."

And in a single, terrible moment I recognised the expression on his face, had seen it too many times before, but by then it was too late. The rifle snapped to his shoulder and he shot her through the head.

13

I OWE my life to Jules Legrande, who shot me down in the same second that Burke killed the girl.

The AK assault rifle packs one and a half tons of muzzle energy when it goes off and the bullet it fires was designed by the Chinese not only to stop a charging Marine, but to lift him off his feet and deposit him a yard to the rear. Which meant that I was flat on my back when Piet Jaeger opened up with his Uzi submachine gun.

Serafino was the only one who got off a shot from the hip as he went down, a lucky one that blew away the top of Legrande's head as far as I could see, but I was already rolling into the cover of the fallen log on the other side of the fire.

The Uzi kicked dirt in a fountain towards me that died abruptly as the magazine emptied and I got to my feet and ran into the trees, head down.

My right arm swung uselessly, blood spurting from a hole in my shoulder. There was no pain, I was too shocked to feel any. That would come later. For the moment I had only one driving passion—to survive.

I stumbled on and behind me there were the cries of the

dying, some confused shouting, and then several bullets passed uncomfortably close, severing branches and twigs above my head.

The Uzi opened up again, Jaeger working it methodically from side to side, slashing a route through the undergrowth. If I stayed where I was, I had a few seconds more to live at the most and that wasn't good enough, not with the bills I had to pay. I swung sharply to the right, forced my way through a screen of bushes and went head-first into the stream.

The icy coldness sharpened me up wonderfully. I surfaced, took a deep breath and went under. If I'd had to rely on my swimming alone I'd have got nowhere. I found it impossible to use my right arm, but the current was fiercer than I had expected and seized me in a grip of iron, pulling me out from the shore so that, when I surfaced again, I found myself in the central channel.

There was a cry from the shore and Jaeger burst through the bushes. He plunged knee-deep into the water and as he raised the Uzi and started to fire, Burke joined him. I went under again and a few moments later the water was rocked by a sudden turbulence, the breath was squeezed from my body and I was lifted bodily.

I was aware of Burke standing there, of his arm moving like a flail, the grenade curving through the air to land a yard away. It was the torrent which saved me, sucking me under into the central passage between great granite slabs so that I had already passed over the smooth apron of rock at the end of the reach and was falling into the pool twenty feet below when the grenade went off.

The water was nine or ten feet deep at that point. I touched bottom, surfaced, and the current swung me across to the other side to ground gently on a shelving bank of black sand beneath a line of overhanging bushes.

In a moment I was into their shelter, still driven by that fantastic reserve of energy that is in us all and which only comes to the fore in periods of real stress and danger. I looked for the densest thicket I could find, crawled into it and lay there shivering.

I discovered that the Smith & Wesson was still with me, thanks to its spring holster, and I got it out awkwardly with my left hand and lay there waiting.

The woods were silent, I was alone in a primeval world, the undergrowth closing in on either hand. Somewhere nearby a bird called sweetly and was answered and then there was the murmur of voices. They seemed to come from another place, to have no connection with me at all, and certainly I made little sense out of what was said.

The only thing I did hear clearly was the sentence "Can you see the body?" delivered in a harsh South African accent that could only belong to Jaeger. It at least meant they thought me dead, presumably killed by the second grenade.

Burke's voice answered, then there was silence. Lying there on my belly I was aware of something digging into my chest and remembered Rosa's parting gift. I unscrewed the top of the flask with my teeth and swallowed. Like liquid fire, the brandy burned its way down and exploded in a warm glow.

There was a single shot, presumably someone being finished off. I lay there and waited, my arm more painful by the minute, and thought of Burke, who had tricked me. No, more than that, had beaten me all along the line. I also considered how I would settle with him. I thought of that a great deal and with variations and drank more brandy and waited.

The waiting game is the hardest one to learn, but it is the only one for a soldier if he wants to survive. Once in the Kasai, I crouched with Burke and four other men in a three-foot trench while the ground above us was raked with heavy machine gun fire. Burke told us we must school ourselves to patience, that to go now would be madness.

But one by one the others cracked, made a run for it and were chopped down. Five hours later when darkness fell, Burke and I crawled away in perfect safety.

My shoulder had stopped bleeding, I think because of my immersion in the ice-cold waters of the stream, and the hole where the bullet had entered had closed into two rather obscene purple lips. And it had gone straight through, thank God, which I discovered when I probed about gingerly with the tips of the fingers of my left hand. The edges of the exit hole seemed to have come together also and although I had obviously lost blood, there was no immediate need to bandage myself up.

I gave it an hour and then started to work my way cautiously through the trees to the top of the apron. I could see the hut, the smoke from the fire, but there was no sign of life.

There was a movement in the bushes over on my right and I crouched, waiting, and then one of the donkeys appeared. A kite called harshly, swooped over the clearing and soared again. He finally went down and perched on the roof of the hut, something he'd never have done if a human had been anywhere around.

That decided me. I stood up and moved cautiously towards the clearing. When I got close, the kite flapped away and left me alone with my dead.

The first body I came to was Legrande's, although he was barely recognisable and was minus his camouflaged jump suit, which they'd presumably taken off him because it would have excited comment.

Serafino and his three friends lay so close together that the sprawling limbs actually touched each other. In death, he smiled savagely, teeth bared, and I judged him to have been shot seven or eight times. The others were in a similar position except for Joe Ricco, who had obviously turned to run and had taken his dose in the back.

I could see it all now quite clearly. The girl had been right. Hoffer had intended her death and had planned it with Burke's connivance. Now he would go to the police, reluctantly tell his story of the kidnapping, of the ransom payment that had failed to secure the girl's return. And the police would have to go through the motions, would lay on their ritual search of the area, as they had done so many times before, expecting Serafino to stay one step ahead as usual, only this time it would be different. This time when they started at the usual place, they would find this butcher's shop, aftermath as the girl had suggested to me earlier, of a fight between rival gangs.

They'd light a few candles in the cathedral in Palermo, Hoffer's friends would commiserate and he'd wipe away a tear with one hand while he was signing the papers that gave him two and a half million with the other.

The girl sprawled partially on one side and, when I turned her over, I sucked in my breath. Her face was a mask of blood, flies settling already. I had seen death in all its obscene variations often enough and yet I sat back on my heels, feeling suddenly faint, overwhelmed by the pity of it all, the tragedy of what had happened to this young girl.

I thought of Burke—of how he had fooled me—fooled me right up to the end, taking Jaeger along with him, even poor, ageing Legrande, presumably on the promise of a larger reward than had ever been suggested to me. Quite a performance when you thought of it. Then something snapped inside and I found myself cursing him wildly out loud.

I think I became wholly Sicilian, the rage boiling over in a torrent of hate. *In this way may I drink the blood of the one who killed you.* Someone had spoken the ancient formula aloud. I gently touched her face, her blood stained my fingers. I raised them to my mouth. It was at that moment that she gave a low moan and stirred.

No one could have been blamed for believing her to be dead. She owed her life to the quantity of blood which had poured down from the wound, covering the face and turning it into a hideous death mask.

The fire was almost out, but the water in the old iron kettle was still warm. I carried it across in my left hand and poured half of it over her face, washing most of the blood away instantly. She moaned, her head moved to one side, then back again.

I crouched, got out my handkerchief, which was soaking wet, and gently sponged the rest of the blood away. The bullet had gouged a furrow in the flesh, starting just above the right temple and continuing along the side of the skull. It was still bleeding, but not a great deal, and the bone showed through.

I had the usual combat medical pack in a side pouch on the right leg and I got it out. The waterproof cover came off in my teeth and exposed the contents—two field dressings and three morphine ampoules in a small plastic box.

I jabbed two of the ampoules into her arm one after the other. She was going to need all the help she could get in the next few hours, because getting her out of here was going to be rough.

I hesitated over the third ampoule, debating whether to use it on myself, but decided against it in the end. I would need all my wits about me and it was a reasonable assumption that the very real pain I was beginning to feel in my shoulder would keep me up to the mark.

I raised her to a sitting position, got a knee behind her and allowed her to sag back against it. There was three feet of bandage on each end of the field dressing and by the time I got it all wound round her head the morphine had done its work. All strain left her face and when I eased her onto her back she looked calm and relaxed.

Only her extreme paleness indicated that something was wrong.

After transferring my holster from my right hip to my left, I managed to bandage my shoulder with the other field dressing rather imperfectly. Then I took the sling from Serafino's M-1 and buckled it about my waist in such a way that my right arm was strapped firmly against my side.

The sun was really beginning to get through the clouds now and when I checked my watch I saw that it was only just coming up to 7 A.M. I got out my copy of the map, which, due to a nylon backing, was still in one piece in spite of its soaking, and had a look at the situation.

Hoffer had said he would wait at a certain map reference on the Bellona road from noon on, which I saw no reason to doubt. Even if he didn't actually turn up in person, someone was certain to be waiting there with transport. With only themselves to worry about, Burke and Piet Jaeger would make excellent time, spurred on no doubt by the thought of a good job well done. In fact it was more than likely that they would reach the rendezvous with time to spare.

In my case I had no option but to make for Bellona and I couldn't see myself doing it in less than six or seven hours and there was always the possibility that my limbs might give out on me on the way, the body refuse to keep going.

I shivered slightly as the sun touched me, conscious for the first time of how wet I was. I got Rosa's flask out and drank a little more brandy. Joanna Truscott lay still and quiet, her arms neatly arranged on either side. She might have been sculpted from marble and resting on top of her own tomb for all the life she showed.

If I left her and pushed myself hard, I might make it to Bellona in five or six hours, always supposing I didn't collapse on the way. Even for a man as efficient as Cerda, it would take an hour or so to get together a rescue party and the return trip back up into the high country would take even longer.

It came down to this then. If I left her, she would lie here alone for fifteen to sixteen hours at the very least and probably longer. By then, she could be dead, which was something I had no intention of allowing to happen. She was going to live and I wanted to be there to see Hoffer's face when he found out.

The animals which earlier had grazed so peacefully, had disappeared, obviously stampeded by the noise of the shooting. There were some bridles hanging by the door. I took one a little way into the woods and finally found a couple of goats and one of the donkeys nibbling a bush together. He allowed me to get the bridle on him with no fuss and I led him back to the clearing and tethered him by the hut.

The animal had obviously been kept to carry in supplies for Serafino and his men, which meant there must be a pack saddle somewhere. I found two inside the hut, both of the same distinctive local pattern, made of wood and leather with a great v-shaped wooden trough in which sacks could be carried.

The brandy had gone to my head and for the moment the pain in my shoulder seemed to have receded a little. I dragged one of the saddles out and managed to heave it onto the donkey's back at the third attempt. God knows what would have happened if the animal had had a temper or turned awkward at all, but it stood there placidly nibbling at the ground as I tightened the girth.

Getting Joanna Truscott up was much more difficult, but after a struggle I managed to get her onto her knees and I knelt in front of her, allowing her to fall across my left shoulder. I deposited her on her back in the wooden trough and none too gently, but she made no sound and lay there, face turned to heaven, her legs dangling on either side of the donkey's rump. I got a blanket from the hut and covered her as well as I could and then tied her into position with a length of old rope.

When I was finished, I was sweating. I sat down and felt for my cigarettes automatically. A wad of sodden paper stained with yellow was all that remained and I crossed to the bodies and found a packet in Ricco's breast pocket, a popular local brand, cheap and nasty, but better than nothing. I smoked one through, had another swallow of Rosa's brandy, then I wrapped the end of the donkey's bridle firmly around my left hand and moved out.

Buddhists believe that if the individual practises meditation long enough he may eventually discover his true self and enter into that state of bliss that eventually leads to Nirvana. At the very least, a kind of withdrawal into the inner self is possible so that the external world fades and time, in its accepted sense, ceases to exist.

The old Jew I had shared a cell with in Cairo had instructed me in the necessary techniques, had saved my life in effect, for I had only survived the Hole because of it. On many occasions I had withdrawn from the world, floated in warm darkness, had surfaced to find a day, two days—even three—had passed and I was still alive.

Stumbling through the wilderness that was Monte Cammarata that morning, I found that something very similar happened. Time ceased to exist, the stones, the sterile valleys and barren hillsides merged with the sky like a picture out of focus and I moved blindly on.

I was conscious of almost nothing. One moment I was stumbling along in front of the donkey, the next a voice said quite plainly: "There are two kinds of people in the world. Pianos and piano players."

Burke had said that to me sitting at a zinc-topped bar in Mawanza. I was drinking warm beer because the electricity supply had been cut and the ice box behind the bar wasn't working, and he was at his eternal coffee, the only thing he would drink in those days. We were half-way through that first contract in Katanga, had lost half our men and were going to lose most of the rest before it was over.

Sitting there at the bar, a machine pistol at my elbow, my face staring back at me from a bullet-scarred mirror, the situation had all the ingredients to hand of every Hollywood adventure film ever made. I remember there was gunfire in the streets, the thud of mortar bombs, and now and again the steady rattle of a heavy machine gun as they tried to clear snipers from the government offices across the square.

By all the rules and because I was not quite twenty years of age it should have been romantic and adventurous, just like an old Bogard movie. It wasn't. I was sick of killing, sick of the brutality, the total inhumanity of it all.

I was at the end of my tether, ready to go straight over the edge, and Burke had sensed it instinctively. He'd started to talk, quietly and calmly. He was enormously persuasive in those days or perhaps it was just that I wanted to believe that he was.

Before he was finished, he had me believing we were on a kind of holy crusade to save the black man from the consequences of his own folly.

"Always remember, Stacey boy, there are two kinds of people in this world. The pianos and the piano players."

An unnecessarily complicated metaphor to suggest that there were those who let it happen and those who did something about it, but at the time I had believed him. In any case, the local police turned against us late that evening and I was too busy trying to save my skin during the week that followed to have time for anything else.

Now, as I stood there on the mountainside, those words floated up from the past to haunt me and, remembering the incident so clearly, I realised, with a kind of wonder, that he hadn't given a damn about me personally; it had been himself he was thinking about as it had always been. He had to straighten me out to his way of thinking because he needed me. Because I had become as essential to him as a gun in his hand. A first-rate deadly weapon. That's what I was—all I had ever been.

I plodded on, the donkey trailing behind, my brain still filled with the past, which meant Burke. His relationship with Piet Jaeger had obviously been different in kind and he had certainly never put a foot wrong that way with me, presumably because his instincts had warned him off.

As I have said, in the beginning he barely tolerated my need for women and my propensity for hard liquor. Now, looking back and remembering how his attitude had changed to a kind of good-humoured acceptance where those things were concerned, I wondered to what extent he had come to realise that their existence made it much easier for him to mould me to his purpose.

We had been on the move now for the best part of four hours and when I stopped to check on the girl's condition she looked exactly the same, but she was still breathing, the only important thing.

For myself, I had moved past pain, floated beyond it as I had done so many times in the Hole. My shoulder existed only as a dull ache, I had forgotten that I had a right arm at all and when the sun clouded over and heavy raindrops spattered the rocks about me, I stumbled on quite cheerfully, Stacey Wyatt, the great survivor.

In late spring or early summer when the first real heat begins, violent thunderstorms are common in the Sicilian high country and occasionally a drenching downpour settles firmly over the mountains for half a day or more.

I think, looking back on it, that it was the rain which saved us. Some people are rainwalkers by nature—it gives them a shot in the arm just to be abroad and feel it beating down on them. I've always been one of that happy band, so the rain-storm which broke over the Cammarata that morning gave me a psychological lift to start with. But there was more to it than that. Suddenly the earth came alive, I was no longer moving through a dead world, there was a freshness to everything.

Perhaps I had become a little delirious, because I found myself singing the famous old marching song of the Foreign Legion that Legrande had taught me a couple of centuries before when we were still brothers, before corruption had set in.

The rain was hammering down now and I went over a rise that blocked the end of a small valley, looked down through the grey curtain and saw Bellona beside the white smear that was the road.

I laughed out loud and shouted to the sky, "I'll have you now, Burke. By God, I'll have you now."

I turned to reach for the donkey's bridle and found that Joanna's head had moved to one side, that her eyes were open. She stared blankly at me for a long moment and then, with infinite slowness, smiled.

I couldn't speak, simply touched her gently on the cheek, took the bridle and stumbled down the hillside, tears of a kind mingling with the rain on my face.

14

THAT FINAL HOUR on the lower slopes was worst of all, for the sparse turf, soaked by the incessant rain, proved difficult to negotiate. I slipped and lost my balance twice, and once the donkey slid to one side, tearing his bridle from my grasp, bringing the heart into my mouth. For a moment it had seemed he would roll over and the result would have been catastrophic.

Joanna Truscott's eyes were closed again and I presumed she had sunk back into unconsciousness. I got a grasp on the donkey's bridle close to the muzzle and started down the next bank, holding his head up with what strength I had left and will-power.

Time again ceased to exist, but now, I suspect, because I had become more than a little light-headed. We floundered down through mud and rain together and, once, I was aware of someone pleading with the donkey in the most reasonable of tones, to stand up like a man and keep going. And then the same voice broke into song again, the same faint trumpet call that had echoed from the Hoggar Mountains of the southern Sahara to the swamps of Indo-China.

I seemed to sink into a well of darkness where nothing existed, only a tiny, flickering point of light at the end of a long tunnel, came out into it blinking and found myself hanging on to the bridle for dear life with both hands.

At what point I had unstrapped my right arm, I don't know. I knew only that I had used it—presumably had needed to—and that blood had soaked through the field dressing.

It was beautiful, the most beautiful colour I had ever seen, vivid against the muted greens and browns of my camouflaged jump suit. The world was a wonderful, exquisite place, the blood mingling with the green and the grey rain falling.

Sheep poured over a bank top like a flood of dirty water and milled around me and, beyond, a ragged shepherd stared, turned and ran along the track towards the village.

I passed the place where I had sat with Rosa, lain with her in a hollow in the sun. Lovely, lovely Rosa who had wanted to warn me, but who was too afraid—afraid of Karl Hoffer.

There was blood below my feet now, which was strange, I shook my head and the stain turned into a red Alfa Romeo in the yard behind Cerda's place two hundred feet below. There was confused shouting, men running along the track towards me.

Once, as a boy, I fell from a tree at the Barbaccia villa and had lain unconscious for an hour until Marco had found me. He looked just the same now, not a day older, which was surprising. The same expression, a mixture of anger and dismay and love. Strange after all those years.

I lay in the mud and he held me up against his knee. "All right—all right now, Stacey."

I clutched at the front of his expensive sheepskin coat. "Hoffer, Marco—Hoffer and Burke. They're mine. You tell Vito that. You tell the *capo*. This is mine—mine alone. My *vendetta!* My *vendetta!*"

I shouted the words out loud and the men of Bellona stood in a silent ring, faces like stone, the Furies in some Greek play awaiting the final bloody outcome with complete acceptance.

The cracks on the ceiling made an interesting pattern, rather like a map of Italy if you looked at it long enough, including the heel, but no Sicily.

Sicily. I closed my eyes, a hundred different things crowding into my mind. When I opened them again, Marco was standing by the bed, hands in the pockets of his magnificent sheepskin coat.

"That's a beautiful coat," I said.

He smiled, the kind of smile I'd known so often as a boy. "How do you feel?"

I was wrapped in a heavy grey blanket. When I opened it I found that I was still in my jump suit, that my shoulder had been rebandaged with what looked like strips of white linen torn from a sheet. I pushed hard and found myself on the edge of the bed, feet on the floor.

"Watch it," Marco warned. "You're lucky to be alive."

"You're wrong," I replied. "Utterly and totally wrong. I'm indestructible. I'm going to live forever."

He wasn't smiling now and when the door opened and Cerda came in quickly, I realised from the expression on his face that I must have shouted.

I saw that the Smith & Wesson was on a small bedside locker, reached for it and held it against my face. The metal was so cold it burned, or that was the sensation. I looked up into their troubled faces and smiled, or thought I did . . .

"Where is she?"

"In my bedroom," Cerda replied.

I was on my feet and lurching through the door, pulling from Marco's outstretched hand. Cerda was ahead of me by some strange alchemy, had the door open and, beyond, the dark, sad woman who was his wife turned from the bed in alarm.

The Honourable Joanna lay quite still, her face the colour of wax, another, cleaner bandage than mine around her head.

I turned to Marco. "What's happening?"

"She's not good, Stacey. I've spoken to the *capo* on the telephone. The nearest doctor is two hours away by road, but he's been instructed to come."

"She mustn't die," I said. "You do understand that?"

"Sure I do, Stacey." He patted my arm. "There's a private ambulance on the way from Palermo, two of the best doctors in Sicily on board. She'll be all right, I've looked at her myself. It's nasty, but it's no death wound. You've nothing to worry about."

"Except Hoffer," I said. "He thinks she *is* dead. For him, it's essential that she is." I looked at him and nodded slowly. "But then you know about that, don't you? All about it?"

He didn't know what to say and tried to smile reassuringly. "Forget Hoffer, Stacey, the *capo* will deal with him. It's all arranged."

"How long for?" I demanded. "A week—a month? He used me, didn't he, Marco? He used me like he uses you and everyone else?" I found that I was still holding the Smith & Wesson in my left hand and pushed it into the holster. "Not any longer. I settle with Hoffer personally."

I turned and looked at the girl. If she was not dead she would be soon, or so I thought at the time. "We'll go now," I told Marco. "In the Alfa. Meet them on the way."

He frowned. "No, better to wait, Stacey. A rough ride in the car after the rain. The surface will have gone on most of the mountain roads."

"He's right," Cerda put in. "If the rain don't stop soon there will be no roads left at all."

"In which case the ambulance will never get up here," I pointed out patiently.

Cerda frowned and turned to Marco, who shrugged helplessly. "Maybe he's got a point."

After that, everything happened in a hurry. They wrapped Joanna in blankets and carried her out to the Alfa in the courtyard, stuffed the well between the rear and front seats with more blankets and laid her across them. I sat in the passenger seat and Cerda leaned in to fasten my seat belt.

"You give my respects to the *capo*, eh?" he said. "Tell him I handled everything just like he told me."

"Sure I will," I said, leaned out of the window and called in English as we drove away, "Up the Mafia—right up!"

But I think the significance of that eloquent and ironic English phrase was completely lost on him.

I was right about the mountain roads and the heavy rain. To say that they dissolved behind our rear wheels may sound like something of an exaggeration, but it was not far from the truth.

I don't suppose we topped twenty miles an hour on the way down; if he'd gone any faster we'd have plunged straight over the edge in places and the Alfa wasn't built to fly.

Not that I was worried. There was a kind of inevitability to everything. The Sicilians are an ancient people and that side came uppermost in me now. Out of some strange foreknowledge, I knew the game was still in play, the climax yet to come. That was inevitable and could not be avoided. Neither by me nor by Burke.

It also helped, of course, to remember that Marco, driving a car sponsored by my grandfather and certain business associates, had once come third in the Mila Miglia.

I closed my eyes and slept. When I opened them again, we were drawn up at the side of the main road beyond Vicari, as I discovered later, and I had lost two hours.

They were already carrying Joanna Truscott into the rear of the ambulance on a stretcher. I tried to get up and found that my legs refused to move and then the door opened and I lurched sideways into the arms of a grey-bearded man in a white coat.

I recall Marco vaguely somewhere in the background, but mainly my friend with the grey beard and the gold-rimmed spectacles. Surprising how respectable a doctor could look—even a Mafia doctor.

Joanna was laid out on the other side, I recall that, and the man leaning over her and then greybeard loomed large again, the interior light shining on his spectacles, the syringe in his hand.

I tried to say no, tried to raise an arm, but nothing seemed to function any longer and then there was that darkness again—we were becoming old friends.

15

BEYOND, through the open french windows, a line of poplars stood like soldiers, waiting for a sign, black against flame, the burned-out fire of day. Long white curtains ballooned in a tiny breeze, ghostlike in the cool darkness of the room. Rebirth is always painful, but my return to life was eased by one of the most beautiful evenings I have ever known.

I was sane again, calm and relaxed, no pain anywhere until I moved and touched off some spark in my right shoulder. There was a nurse at the end of the bed reading a book by the light of a small table lamp. She turned at my movement, the starched white cap like the halo around the face of a Madonna. When she leaned over me, her hand on my forehead was cooler than anything I had ever known.

She left, closing the door quietly. It reopened almost at once and greybeard came in.

"How do you feel?" he asked in Italian.

"Alive again. A remarkably pleasant sensation. Where am I?"

"The Barbaccia villa."

He switched on the bedside lamp and took my pulse, composed and grave. The inevitable stethoscope was produced and probed around in the area of my chest for a while.

He nodded, to himself, of course, and stuffed it back into his pocket. "Your shoulder—it pains you?"

"A little—when I move."

Behind him the door opened. I could sense his presence even before I became aware of the distinctive aroma of his Havana and then he moved into the light, his face dark and brooding, calm as always, Cesare Borgia sprung to life again, eternal and indestructible.

"Do you think you'll ever die?"

As if following my thought processes perfectly, he smiled. "So, he's going to live on us, this grandson of mine, eh, Tasca?"

"Oh, he will survive the bullet, although much work will be needed on the shoulder if he is not to suffer some permanent stiffening." Dr. Tasca looked down at me in a kind of mild reproof. "You should not have used the arm, young man. That was unfortunate."

I didn't bother to argue and he turned back to my grandfather. "No, it is his general condition that worries me. Physically speaking he is balanced on the edge of a precipice. A slight nudge and he goes straight down."

"Hear that?" My grandfather just prevented himself from prodding me with his stick. "You want to die young, eh?"

"Can you make me a better offer?"

I tried to sound gay and flippant, but Tasca obviously didn't approve at all. "I understand you have been in prison."

I nodded. "Of a kind—Egyptian labour camp variety."

"With the chain gang?" His face for the first time registered some kind of concern. "Now we know." He turned again to my grandfather. "When he is on his feet he must come to me for a thorough examination, *capo*. He would well have tubercular lesions and there are definite signs of incomplete recovery from blackwater fever which could mean kidney damage. Not only will he need treatment, but careful nursing and rest—several months of complete inactivity."

"Thank you, Doctor Kildare," I said. "You've made my day."

Tasca looked completely mystified by the remark, but in any event my grandfather dismissed him. "Back to the girl now. I want to talk to my grandson alone."

To my shame, it was only then that I consciously gave her a thought. "You've got Joanna Truscott here too? How is she?"

He pulled a chair forward and sat down. "She's doing all right, Stacey. Tasca's a specialist in brain surgery—the best in Sicily. He brought a portable x-ray unit with him and gave her a thorough examination. She's lucky—the skull isn't even fractured. She'll have a bad scar, probably for life, but a good hairdresser can fix that."

"Shouldn't she have gone to a hospital?"

He shook his head. "No need. She couldn't have better treatment if she did and it's safer here."

I tried to sit up, my stomach hollow. "Hoffer knows then?"

He pushed me gently back against the pillow. "Only that his stepdaughter is dead. Not officially, of course, so that the world can be told, but he's spoken to me already on the telephone."

"And told you?"

He shook his head. "He asked for a General Council meeting tonight. He's due here in half an hour."

"I don't understand," I said. "What General Council?"

"Did you think I was Mafia all on my own, Stacey?" He laughed. "Sure, I'm *capo—capo* in all Sicily, but the big decisions are made by the Council. We have the rules and they have to be obeyed. Even I can't break them." He shrugged. "Without the rules we are nothing."

The Honoured Society. I shook my head. "All right, maybe I'm not thinking too clearly, but I still don't see what Hoffer is doing coming here."

"First you tell me what happened in the mountains. We go on from there."

"Are you trying to tell me you don't know?"

"Some only. Now be a good boy and do as I say."

So I told him, in detail, including my various suspicions about things from the beginning and he took it all without a sign, even my deliberately graphic description of the massacre.

When I was finished, he sat there in silence for a moment. "Why did you go, Stacey, that is what I can't understand? You knew this man Burke was not being honest with you, you distrusted Hoffer, you knew that even I was not telling you the whole truth and yet still you went."

"God knows," I said, and, thinking about it in retrospect, I honestly couldn't explain it even to myself. "Some kind of death wish, I suppose."

The words were my own and yet, at their saying, every instinct in me rebelled. "No, to hell with it. It was Burke —always Burke. Something between us that I can't put into words, even for myself. Something I had to prove. I can't say more than that."

"You hate this man, I think? This is the truth of it."

I thought about that for a while and said slowly, "No, more than hate—much more. He took me with him into a dark world of his own creating, made me into what I am not, moulded me to his purpose. Up there on the mountain he told me he is a sick man, some kind of oblique explanation for his behavior. I think he was trying to find in it an excuse for his own conduct, but he lies even to himself. He was in decay long before his lungs started to rot. He needed no excuse."

"Ah, now I perceive a glimmer of light," he said. "You hate him for being something other than you previously thought he was."

He was right, of course, but only partially so. "You could have something there. In the early days when I first met him, he seemed the only really substantial thing in a world gone mad. I believed in him completely."

"And later? What happened later?"

"Nothing." I shook my head. "I was the one who changed, he didn't. He was always what he is now, that's the terrible thing. The Sean Burke I thought I knew in Lourenco Marques, and after, never actually existed."

The silence enveloped us and I lay there thinking about it all. Finally I looked up at him again. "You knew what they intended, didn't you?"

"In part only and guessed the rest. Hoffer was deported from the States some years ago after a prison sentence for tax evasion. He worked with Cosa Nostra, then came to us here in Sicily with several of his old American-Sicilian Mafia associates. They brought in new ideas as I told you. Drugs, prostitution, other kinds of vice. I didn't want them, but they were all Mafia."

"Once in, never out?"

"That's right. The Council said they were entitled to be in."

"So you took them?"

He nodded. "Mostly they were good administrators, I'll say that for them. Hoffer, for example, took over the running of our oil interests at Gela. On the face of it, he did a good job, but I never trusted him—or his associates."

"And these were the men who worked against you?"

"Nothing is as simple as that. Sometimes together, often individually, they would give me trouble. They thought it would be easy, that they could fast-talk the stupid old Sicilian peasant into the ground. Take over. When that failed, they tried other methods."

"Including the bomb that killed my mother? You knew they intended to kill you if possible and still you worked with them?" I shook my head. "Sharks—tearing each other to pieces at the smell of blood."

"Still you don't see." He sighed. "The Council is Mafia, Stacey, not Vito Barbaccia alone. The rules said they were entitled to be in. The other business was personal."

"And you killed them all according to the rules, is that what you're trying to tell me?"

"Any one of them could have been behind the bomb that killed your mother—or all of them."

"Then why is Hoffer still around?"

"Drop by drop is better. I have my own way of doing things," he said grimly. "Hoffer is a very stupid man, like all men who think they are clever. He married this English widow, this aristocrat, for her money. Unfortunately she was smarter than he realised and soon sized him up for what he really was. She wouldn't give him a penny."

"Why didn't she leave him?"

"Who knows with a woman? Love, perhaps. So he eased her out of this world into the next with a carefully contrived accident—he still doesn't realise that I know about that, by the way—then discovered she had left him nothing."

"Everything to Joanna."

"Exactly, except that under the terms of the trust he was next in line if the girl died before coming into her inheritance. Once she came of age, he was finished. She could make a will on the spot, leave it to charity or some obscure cousin—anything. No point in even killing her then."

He got to his feet and moved to the window and stood there, a dark shadow again. "But he wasn't simply motivated by greed in his desire to lay hands on his stepdaughter's fortune. He was afraid. He faced a death sentence. He used our money, Mafia money, in various bullion deals, mainly in Egypt, hoping to make a personal killing. Unfortunately someone tipped off the authorities. On two occasions his boats were caught red-handed."

"Someone informed the authorities? Someone called Vito Barbaccia?" I laughed until I started to choke and he hurried to my bedside and poured water into a glass. I gulped some down and handed the glass back to him. At least I'd made him look anxious.

"It's really damned ironic, isn't it?" I told him. "Didn't you know that I was in one of those boats? That that's how I came to be in an Egyptian prison?"

For once in his life I'd stopped him cold. A hand stretched out towards me, there was utter dismay on his face. "Stacey," he stammered. "What can I say? I did this to you."

"Forget it," I said. "It's too funny to be tragic. Now let me have the next thrilling installment."

He sank down into his chair again, obviously still shaken. "All right. Hoffer had to have his chance to recoup so that the Society shouldn't suffer. The Council met to consider his case. He confessed frankly, but tried to make out that the deals had been intended to benefit the Society. Not that it did him any good. Even if that was the truth, he'd had no authority from the Council to proceed. He admitted his liability and asked for time to get the money together."

"And time was given?"

"There was no reason to refuse. He told the Council that under the terms of his wife's will, he had been left substantial business interests in America. That he could realise these within two or three months and have more than enough money to put things right."

"And the Council believed him?"

"Why should he lie? If he didn't come up with the money he would be taken care of, no matter where he tried to run."

"But you knew he was lying?"

He nodded tranquilly. "The true measure of Hoffer's stupidity lies in the fact that he can't accept that an old Sicilian peasant is smarter than he is. I've always been one step in front of him—always. I saw a photostat of his wife's will, even before he knew the terms."

"Why didn't you tell the Council?"

"I was interested. I wanted to see what he would come up with."

"And be one step ahead of him as usual? You knew that his solution was to get rid of his stepdaughter before she came of age?"

"Let us say that after having seen the actual will, it had occurred to me as a likely possibility. Later, I got wind of the business with Serafino, of how it had gone wrong."

"And then I turned up and brought you up to date." I was getting angry again. "If you knew the girl was with Serafino because she wanted to stay out of Hoffer's way till her birthday, you must have known that the purpose of our little foray into the mountains, as outlined to me, was a lie. That the only reason there could possibly be for going in there was to destroy her." My voice had risen slightly. "What in the hell did you think was going to happen when we got there and I found out, or did you think I was lying to you? Did you think I'd become a murderer of young girls?"

"Don't be stupid, Stacey," he said coldly. "You are my flesh—I know you. That kind of deed we leave to the Hoffers and the Burkes of this world. Men without honour."

"Honour?" I laughed wildly. "Didn't you realise that Burke would have to kill me because he knew I'd never stand by and see them murder the girl? That you, by your silence, were sending me to my death as surely as Hoffer?"

"But I had no choice, don't you see?" He said patiently.

"Listen and try to understand, Stacey. The Council gave Hoffer time—time to recoup their money, and how he did that was of no particular concern. They expected either cash on the barrel on the due date or his head—nothing less. But once a member has been given time he is entitled to follow his operation through without interference from within the Society. If I had warned you that he intended to have the girl killed, urged you to prevent it, I would have been guilty of breaking one of the oldest of Mafia laws."

"Death at last for Vito Barbaccia, is that what you are saying?"

"Death?" He seemed genuinely surprised. "You think that frightens me? But I thought I had made it clear to you. The rules are there for all to obey, even the *capo*. Without them we are nothing. They are the strength of the Society, the reason we have survived. Oh no, Stacey, he who breaks the rules deserves to die—must die."

It occurred to me for the briefest of moments that I might be going out of my head. I was moving into an unknown country now with attitudes and rules of behaviour as archaic and formalised as a Court of Chivalry in the Middle Ages.

Thinking was an effort, but I managed to say, "It still doesn't hang together. I didn't know Hoffer was Mafia, but he knew I was your grandson and I made it clear to Burke that I had discussed our mission with you."

"But why should that worry him? The story of his step-daughter's kidnapping was acceptable enough, including his reasons for handling it quietly and the thought that his story about the money from the trust fund had been accepted by everyone including me. What could this affair of the Truscott girl have to do with that?"

Which made enough sense to get by. Certainly it was as acceptable an explanation as anything else that had been offered to me in this nightmare world of Mafia politics.

"Which still leaves us with the fact that you could have warned me," I said slowly. "You could have given me some kind of an idea of what was going on, told me at least that Hoffer was Mafia on that first night when I discussed things with you."

"Only by breaking our law, Stacey, and that I could not do. Hoffer knew that and I had everything to gain by remaining silent. It was Hoffer who brought you into the affair, Hoffer and this man Burke who lied to you. If you turned against them, Hoffer could blame no one but himself."

"This Council of yours might have other ideas," I said. "They might find it difficult to believe that your grandson wasn't working under your direct orders."

"Which remains to be seen," he said. "But you must come to the meeting, Stacey, and see for yourself. It should be rather amusing."

"Amusing!" If I had been close enough I think I might have struck him at that moment. "I could have been killed up there, don't you understand? I loved you—I've always loved you in spite of everything and you sent me to my death without a word for the sake of a few stupid archaic rules—a game for schoolboys with no sense to it."

He frowned. "To your death, Stacey, you really believe that?" He laughed harshly. "Yes, all right. I was going to keep you out that first night when you came to see me, by force if necessary. But then I talked to my grandson—saw him in action, saw him for what he was, *mafioso* just like his grandfather, only better. And this Burke, this hollow man, this dead thing walking with the grave stench already on him—you think I believe my grandson couldn't handle him?"

His voice had dropped to a hoarse whisper and he leaned close to me, one hand on the edge of the bed to support his weight. I stared at him, hypnotised.

"Don't you see, Stacey? Hoffer had to have his chance,

the rules said so, but I wanted him flat on his belly grovelling because I believed that, of all of them, he was the man most likely to be responsible for the death of my daughter. I wanted his scheme to fail so I allowed the best, the most ruthless *mafioso* I have ever known to wreck it for me."

A wave of greyness soured my body and I shivered as he sat back and calmly lit another cigar. "It's just a game to you, isn't it? The more complicated the better. You could have had Hoffer's head blown off at any time you wanted. At home—in the street, but that wouldn't have been good enough. It had to be a classical drama."

"They always last longer." He stood up, his face calm, flicked ash from a lapel and adjusted his tie. "They'll be here soon. I'll send Marco with some clothes for you."

The door closed behind him, I stared up at the ceiling blankly for a moment, then swung my legs to the floor, stood up and tried to walk.

I made it to the french windows, turned and went back. I was more than a little light-headed and my shoulder hurt like hell when I moved it, but at least I could get around, which was all I needed.

I was rummaging through the drawers of the dressing table when Marco came in. He dropped a suede jacket, whipcord pants and a white nylon shirt on the bed and produced the Smith & Wesson.

"Is this what you are looking for?"

He tossed it across. I pulled it from its holster, hefted it for a moment in my left hand, then swung the cylinder to one side and spilled the cartridges onto the coverlet.

I reloaded it carefully, snapped the cylinder home and pushed it back into its holster. "There was a wallet."

"That also."

He produced it from his pocket and gave it to me, making no comment when I checked the contents.

"Are they here?"

"Most of them."

"And Hoffer?"

"Not yet."

I discovered that my hands were trembling slightly. "Help me get dressed. We mustn't keep them waiting."

16

THEY MET in the salon and I sat in a wicker chair on the terrace behind a vine-covered trellis, Marco at my shoulder, and watched.

I had a perfect view and the acoustics were excellent. There were eight of them, including my grandfather, and in appearance they were a pretty assorted bunch. Three of them were real old-style *capos*, carelessly dressed in deliberately shabby clothes. A fourth had taken off his coat, exposing cheap and gaudy braces. The others were all wearing expensive lightweight suits, although no one could approach my grandfather's magnificence, sitting there at the head of the table in the cream lightweight suit he had worn on that first evening.

Hoffer wore dark glasses, presumably an affectation, and nodded soberly at what was said to him by the man on his right. He looked composed enough and I wondered what was going on in his mind.

My grandfather lifted a small silver bell and at its ring the low buzz of conversation was instantly stilled. Every head turned towards him and he let the silence hang for a moment before saying, "Karl Hoffer asked for this meeting specially. I don't know what he's going to say any more than you do, but I guess we all know what it's about, so let's listen."

Hoffer didn't get up. He seemed calm, but when he removed his dark glasses for a moment, he looked tired, and, when he started to talk, the voice was grave and subdued. Altogether a most convincing performance.

"When I faced the Council some months back in order to explain my conduct in certain unfortunate business transactions, I promised to repay the Society every penny of the money lost owing to my imprudence. I asked for six months, time enough for me to realise certain assets in the States left to me by my late wife. I know some of you here thought I was still buying time, that the Society would never see its money. Others, thank God, were willing to trust me."

That remark on any other occasion would have been enough to make me laugh out loud. There wasn't a man at that table who would have trusted his neighbour for more than five minutes at any one time outside the rigid framework of Mafia law.

They knew it and Hoffer knew it, unless—and this seemed incredible—he really was so stupid as to think them a bunch of unwashed Sicilian peasants he could walk over whenever he pleased.

"Have you come to tell us you can't pay, Karl?"

There was an edge of malice in my grandfather's voice and he spoke with ill-concealed eagerness. Even Hoffer's performance paled by comparison with this one.

"Why no, Vito." Hoffer turned to him, the dark glasses back in place again. "I'd have been in a position to settle within the period granted, or so my American lawyers tell me. As it happens, owing to an"—he hesitated, then continued with obvious difficulty—"to an unfortunate, and for me personally, most tragic happening, I am now in a position to be able to assure the Council that replacing the Society's money lost through my negligence is now the least of my worries."

He certainly got a reaction from most of them. There was a stir, a murmur of voices, and then my grandfather raised his hand. "Maybe you'd better explain, Karl."

Hoffer nodded. "It's simple enough. As you all know, my dear wife died in a car crash in France a little while back. Quite naturally, she left the very considerable fortune inherited from her first husband, in trust for her daughter, Joanna. Under the terms of that trust, I was to inherit if the girl failed to reach her majority." He clasped his hands together, knuckles showing white, looked down at the table. "Even now I found it hard to believe, but I have it on the most reliable authority that my stepdaughter met her death in the area of Monte Cammarata this morning under the most tragic circumstances."

If there is one thing a Sicilian loves it is a good story and by this time Hoffer had them by the throat.

"My stepdaughter was kidnapped some weeks ago by a bandit many of you know only too well—Serafino Lentini."

The man in the braces spat on the floor at the name and there was a general stir.

"I didn't come to the Council with my trouble because I knew it couldn't help. As we all know, Serafino Lentini was no friend to the Society, even though he's been used as a *sicario* on one or two occasions."

"You speak of him in the past tense, Karl," my grandfather remarked. "May we take it that is where he now belongs?"

"The only good news I bring the Council tonight," Hoffer said. "The police, as we all know, are helpless in these affairs, so when Lentini sent a message demanding ransom, I scraped the necessary amount together, met him myself as stipulated on the Bellona road. He took the money and laughed in my face when I asked for my stepdaughter. He had decided to keep her for himself."

"Strange," my grandfather cut in smoothly. "I had always understood that Serafino lacked some of the essential equipment necessary to a Don Juan."

Hoffer paused, glancing at him sharply, and countered with exactly the right remark. "It was not me he was attacking in behaving in this way. He was showing his contempt for the Society—for all of us." He shrugged and spread his arms wide. "I couldn't sit back and do nothing while the wretched girl suffered untold indignities at the hands of his men. In the past I have had the occasion to use the services of an Irish soldier-of-fortune, a Colonel Burke, well known for his exploits as a mercenary in the Congo. It seemed to me that a man of his stamp might be able to do what no one else could—penetrate the fastnesses of the Cammarata and bring my stepdaughter to safety. I flew to Crete where I met Burke, who agreed to take on this hazardous undertaking with the assistance of three men who had served under him in the Congo."

He'd even get me interested now and the silence in the salon wouldn't have been out of place in a cathedral cloister.

"It was when Colonel Burke and his men arrived that I discovered an amazing thing. One of them was the *capo's* grandson, a young man named Wyatt."

The ball was well into Barbaccia's court. He caught it neatly, had, I suspected, been waiting for it.

He coughed and managed to look serious. "You all know my daughter and her son came to live with me after her American husband was killed in Korea. She died as the direct result of the action of some filthy assassin who had intended to end my days. Unfortunately my grandson blamed me in part for what had happened to his mother." It was obviously the night for the baring of souls. "We became estranged and the boy, then aged nineteen, ran away. I lost sight of him for some time, then learned he was serving in the Congo as a mercenary. He came to see me the other night with this man Burke and told me why they were in Sicily. I was astonished at his story because I couldn't understand why Karl had not come to me for help, but I presumed he had his reasons."

"Help?" Hoffer spread his arms again, appealing to the assembled Council. "How could anyone help? My only hope lay in Burke and his men." And then, as if it had only just occurred to him, he turned rather uncertainly to Barbaccia. "I had nothing to hide. It seemed to me under the circumstances that the fewer who knew about the affair, the better for the girl's sake."

"No question of that." My grandfather nodded. "After all, my grandson gave me a full account of what they intended to do. Parachute into the Cammarata—a daring conception."

By now, of course, the atmosphere had changed and there was not a man there who didn't realise that beneath the surface something special was going on between Hoffer and my grandfather.

"I'm sorry the girl was killed," Barbaccia said. "I know she was close to you, Karl. To lose a daughter gives more than pain. I know."

"*Capo!*" Hoffer's voice was hoarse. "God knows how, but I must tell you. In the fight—the gunfight between Colonel Burke's party and Serafino's men—your grandson also met his end, dying I understand in a vain attempt to save my stepdaughter's life."

I saw it all then, the reason for Hoffer's performance, his detailed account of the whole affair leading up to this final devastating blow delivered in public before everyone who counted.

My grandfather shrivelled, dropped his stick, became an old man in an instant. "Stacey?" he said hoarsely. "Stacey is dead?"

Hoffer didn't actually smile in triumph, but even he

couldn't control the tiniest quiver at the corner of his mouth. My grandfather chose that precise moment to descend. He produced a fresh cigar and struck a match, his old self again.

"Very good, Karl, excellent. You could have gone a long way in the Society if only you hadn't been so stupid."

Marco tapped me on the shoulder, but I was already on my feet and moving into the salon. There was no thunderclap as Jove descended from heaven, but the result was about the same.

Hoffer had gone very pale, mostly from shock, but also, I suppose, at the instant realisation that his goose was cooked. To the others I was simply an intruder and the fattest, most harmless-looking man there produced a Mannlicher automatic with all the speed of a real pro.

My grandfather waved him down. "My grandson, Stacey Wyatt, gentlemen, who, according to our friend here, died gallantly on Cammarata this morning in a vain attempt to save the life of Joanna Truscott, As a matter of interest, that young lady is under medical care in another part of the villa at this very moment."

Hoffer's hand dropped to his pocket and death stared out at him from the Smith & Wesson in my left hand.

"No, Stacey! Not here. Here he is inviolate," my grandfather called. "It is the law."

The gentleman in the flashy braces relieved Hoffer of a Walther and I pushed the Smith & Wesson back into its holster.

"And now, the truth, my friends." Barbaccia snapped a finger and Marco, who had moved in behind me, took a grey document from an envelope, unfolded it and laid it on the table.

"A photostat of the will Hoffer referred to which only came into my hands this afternoon." I wondered how many of them believed that. "It is in English, but there are enough of you here who understand that language to satisfy the Council that Hoffer lied. That his wife left him nothing. That there were no business assets in America that he could realise to fulfill his debt to us." He looked at Hoffer. "Would you deny this?"

"Go to hell!" Hoffer told him.

My grandfather continued, "His one hope was to murder the girl, but Lentini double-crossed him. So he tried this man Burke. But they needed someone who knew the country, spoke the language, and Burke produced my grandson. My grandson, who believed until the very moment that he was shot down in cold blood together with Serafino and the girl; believed as I did until I read this will and heard his story, that he was on the mountain to save the girl. By the grace of God and the incompetence of this man Burke, he survived and managed to get the girl to Bellona."

There was nothing Hoffer could say, nothing that would do him the slightest good with the hard-faced gentry standing around that table. He answered in the only way his animal nature would allow, striking to hurt.

"All right, Barbaccia, you win. But I put the bomb that killed your daughter in your car. With my own hands."

He spat in my grandfather's face. Marco took a quick step forward, my grandfather's hand flattened against his chest. "No, Marco, leave it. He is a dead man walking." He wiped his face with a handkerchief and dropped it on the floor. "The man Burke. He is at your villa?"

Hoffer, blaming Burke, I suspect, more than himself for his downfall, nodded.

"Good. Now get out! Outside the gate you are on your own."

Hoffer turned and lurched towards the french windows. He was crossing the terrace when I caught up with him, but as I swung him around, Marco already had me by the arm, my grandfather just behind him, moving with amazing speed for a man of his age.

"No, Stacey, not here. Here at the Council meeting he is inviolate. It is the law. Break it and you die too."

"To hell with your bloody laws," I said and he slapped me across the face.

I staggered back and Hoffer laughed shrilly. "That's good—I like that. That's what I gave Rosa Solazzo last night, Wyatt, only more. She wanted to warn you, you didn't know that, did you? I don't know what you did to her, but that stupid bitch must have liked it."

I tried to get at him, and Marco and two of the others held me back. "Want to know what I did with her?" He laughed again. "I gave her to Ciccio. He always panted for her. The original bull that one. He'll have tried every variation known to man by now and a few of his own thrown in for fun."

He wanted to hurt and he succeeded. I called him every dirty name I'd ever known and they held me there as he went through the garden to his Mercedes parked outside the gate. It was only when he started up and drove away that my grandfather ordered them to release me. I turned and pushed my way through the group and went back to my room.

I stood there in the darkness, my shoulder throbbing, sweat soaking the nylon shirt, and thought of Rosa. Poor Rosa. *So, she'd decided to stop being afraid after all and had left it too late*. I remembered what Hoffer had said about Ciccio and at the thought of that animal sweating over her, I cracked completely. The only decent thing in this whole stinking business as far as I was concerned had been that girl's futile gesture in trying to save me. I went out through the french windows on the run and moved through the gardens to the courtyard at the rear.

There was a choice of three cars in the garage, but I took Marco's red Alfa mainly because it had automatic gears and would be easier to manage with one hand. The fact that he'd left his keys on show also helped.

They must have heard me go the moment I rounded the house, but the gatekeeper was standing in the door of the lodge and recognised me as I arrived. The gates opened a split second later, too late for Marco who came down the drive on the run and still had ten yards to go as I took the Alfa into the night with a surge of power.

About three miles outside Palermo, I saw flames in the night and several cars blocking the road. I braked and pulled in behind a slow-moving line of vehicles that was being waved on by a policeman on the wrong side.

Petrol spilled across the road, burning fitfully, and beyond, where it had crashed head-on into the concrete retaining wall, a Mercedes saloon blazed fiercely.

I leaned out of the window as I approached the policeman. "What happened to the driver?"

"What do you think?"

He waved me on and I moved into the night. So that was Mafia justice? Swift and certain and my grandfather had had his revenge. But the rest was mine—the rest was my *vendetta*. No one on earth was going to cheat me of that.

17

IT WAS still Holy Week in Palermo, something I had forgotten, and the streets were crowded, mainly with family groups. Everyone seemed to be enjoying themselves and, when it started to shower, no one took the slightest notice.

The municipal fireworks display got going just as I turned into the Via Vittorio Emanuele and drove towards the cathedral, gigantic coloured flowers blossoming in the night, and all around me I saw that strange mixture of carnival and piety so peculiar to Sicily.

There was little traffic, for this was a night for walking, but progress was slow, as in most cases the crowd simply flooded out from the pavements into the centre of the street.

I was sweating again and still conscious of the lightheadedness I'd noticed earlier. Perhaps it was the drugs I'd had or maybe I was simply perilously close to being at the end of my resources. Whatever the reason, I felt like an outsider looking in, alienated from everything around me.

It was a nightmare scene that needed a Dante to do it justice. The noise of the fireworks, the multitude of exploding colours, the voice of the crowd, and beyond, the penitents in sackcloth, bare-footed in the rain, three at the front of the procession staggering under the Cross, Our Lady floating in the darkness above the flaring torches.

The chanting swelled until it filled my head like the sea, whips, rising above the heads of the crowd, cracked symbolically as they descended. The stench of incense, of hot candlegrease was nauseating, almost more than I could bear, and then the tail of the procession passed, the crowd parted and I moved on.

I put the window down, breathed deeply on the fresh damp air and gave some thought to the situation which faced me at the villa.

First there would be the man on the gate with his automatic rifle and no other way in unless I could climb over that fifteen-foot concrete wall, which didn't seem likely with one arm out of commission. In the villa itself, the two houseboys. I could discount them for a start and the kitchen staff, which left Ciccio, Piet Jaeger and Burke. Against them on my side, I had my left hand, the Smith & Wesson and five rounds in the chamber. Enough, considering the mood I was in.

Any professional gunman is faced with two kinds of killing. The first is in hot blood, an instant heat generated by a particular situation, usually in defence of his own life or his employer's.

The second is a different proposition altogether, a cool, calculating business where the situation is carefully assessed, the risks worked out in advance. But even that isn't enough. The mental preparation is just as important, the winding-up of the whole personality like a clock spring so that when the moment comes there is an instant readiness to kill.

In the final analysis, that's what separates the real professional from the rest of the field. A willingness to kill without the slightest hesitation, something most people can never hope to do.

But I could. Stacey Wyatt could. Had done it enough times before, would do it tonight and probably again. Strange how the thought, the possibility of my own death, never occurred to me, just as it never occurs to the professional criminal that he might get caught on his next job.

I slowed and paused briefly because of traffic congestion where the bridge crosses the Fiume Oreto on the Messina road. My face was hot, probably a fever starting, and I put my head out into the rain. It was cool and refreshing and then a strange thing happened. For a brief moment, for an instant in time, the sounds of the traffic faded, all sounds in fact except for the rain swishing through the trees on the other side of the road, and it was like nothing I'd ever known before and the scent of the wisteria in the garden of the house beyond filled the night, unbearable in its sweetness.

It was a fragile moment, broken by a peremptory horn behind, and I drove on, pulled back into some kind of reality. But was that true? Who was I? What in the hell was all this about? What was I doing here?

When I ran from Sicily at my mother's death, I ran from a lot of things. From pain, I suppose, and out of revulsion at the cruelty of life. And from my grandfather whom I loved deeply and who now stood revealed as a monster who battened on the misery of the poor and ordered death with the certainty of God.

But in running from Barbaccia's grandson, I was also fleeing from the boy the Wyatts of Wyatt's Landing had refused to accept. I was running from the Stacey Wyatt that life and circumstance had made me.

And I had a chance to find myself—my own true self—me and no one else. For a time it had worked, had gone well. I had made it to Mozambique and Lourenco Marques, could have made it further and arrived at some kind of destination under my own steam, knowing myself as far as anyone can hope to or at least knowing what I could do on my own.

But for me there had been the Lights of Lisbon. I had met Sean Burke, had become another kind of Stacey Wyatt, and that was very much that until the Hole. I suppose most men have their Lights of Lisbon, but only a few know the Hole. Well, I had come to know it well, had been in filth and darkness, had survived, had found another Stacey Wyatt, someone I'd never known before who asked questions—asked questions about a lot of things.

My return to Sicily had been not only inevitable but essential, I saw that now. I had to see again that incredible figure so much a part of my youth, Vito Barbaccia, Lord of Life and Death, *capo mafia* in all Sicily, my grandfather, who kept telling me I was *mafioso* just like him only better and who, in my heart, I knew already saw me at the head of the Council table when he was gone.

But he was wrong. I wasn't the man Burke had created, the hired killer posing as a soldier, and I wasn't my grandfather's version either. To hell with both of them.

Who was I then? I had gone into the mountains, eyes open, knowing the situation was not what it seemed, with some vague notion of beating Burke at his own game, whatever that game was. I had lost, but so had he. Beat him now I had to, on his terms and on his own ground if ever I was to be free. However bloody that encounter might prove, however savage the prospect, it could not be evaded. I had stood in his shadow too long.

A fierce anger flooded through me then and as I swept round the next bend and found myself in the final stretch, Hoffer's villa floodlight in the night three hundred yards up the road, a kind of madness took possession of me. I put my foot down hard and took the Alfa into the night with a burst of power, the engine howling like a wolf.

The guard saw me coming, but by the time he realised

my intention, there was nothing to be done. He started to
unsling his automatic rifle, thought better of it and jumped
for his life as the Alfa ripped the bronze gates from their
hinges and continued up the drive.

What happened next was very much the fortunes of
war, the unexpected that decides who wins or loses. A
Lambretta came round the bend of the drive, slowly, because the rider had obviously only just started. I braked
instinctively, swung the wheel over with my one good hand
and slid broadside into the shrubbery in a wave of gravel.

The Lambretta too had skidded as the rider braked
desperately, spinning in a circle so that the machine halted
pointing the way it had come. It was one of the houseboys
dressed in his best, obviously ready for an evening on the
town. As I scrambled out of the Alfa, the Smith & Wesson
ready in my left hand, I caught a glimpse of his white,
terrified face, and then he gunned the engine and roared
out of sight, back towards the villa.

I could have had him with no trouble, but this wasn't
his affair and I let him go, even though it meant he would
arouse the house, that Burke and Jaeger would know who
it was. Perhaps the truth is that I wanted them to know. I
didn't get time to consider, because a couple of bullets
pumped into the Alfa as the gate guard arrived, and I ran
for cover.

My right arm was hurting like hell, but the pain sharpened me, made me come alive again. It was raining harder
now and I crouched in the bushes and waited as I had
waited in other places, other jungles than this, for the
slightest rustle, the breaking of a twig.

By some process of association the Lagona operation
came back to me when we had parachuted in and brought
out the nuns from their beleaguered mission. It had been a
bad time, the beginning of the rains and thick bush all the
way. And then I remembered, for some strange reason,
that Burke had wanted to go in by armoured convoy. I'd

been the one who suggested the drop and he'd objected because we would have no vehicles to come out in. But I had pointed out that we would have surprise on our side on our way back, fighting our way through them before they'd realised we'd even been in.

And in the end, he had agreed, as he always did, and at the first briefing it had somehow become his own idea. How many times had that happened? How many times right through to the Cammarata?

It had been staring me in the face for years and I had not seen it before, blinded by my belief in the man, and I was aware of a strange release of tension, almost as if I had been set free from something, a kind of fierce joy surging through me.

I am Stacey Wyatt and no one else. That thought echoed in my head as a twig snapped. Several things happened. Somewhere in the night a voice called up on the roof and I picked up a stone and tossed it into the bushes. My friend of the gate was no bargain whatever Hoffer had paid him. He jumped out of the shrubbery and fired several times where my stone had landed.

I shot him through the upper part of his right arm, he cried out and spun round, dropping his rifle. We faced each other in the rain, the statue of some Greek goddess behind him watching blindly. There was no fear in his eyes. Perhaps Hoffer had made a better bargain than he knew.

"If you want to live, talk," I told him. "What happened to Signorina Solazzo?"

"She's been locked in her room all day."

"And Ciccio? Is Ciccio with her?"

"He has been." He shrugged. "I don't know. It's nothing to do with me. She has the room with the gold door on the second floor." He gripped his arm tightly to arrest the flow of blood. "Ciccio told me you and the Frenchman were dead."

"He was wrong, wasn't he? The others are here."

"Somewhere about."

I nodded. "Hoffer is dead. Barbaccia caught up with him at last. Go now—what happens here has nothing to do with you."

He faded into the bushes as a rifle cracked, the unmistakable thud of an AK, and a bullet chipped a piece out of the Greek statue's head. As I went to one knee, someone dropped back out of sight behind the retaining wall up there in the Moorish roof garden.

I called softly, "It's me, Sean—Stacey. I'm coming up."

There was no reply, but the floodlights which dotted the garden were dowsed suddenly. I don't know whose bright idea that was, but it suited me perfectly. I moved out at once through the welcome darkness, scrambled over the low wall of the ground-floor terrace and went into the lounge through the open french window.

The hall was a place of shadows dimly lit by a single lamp, but I had to keep moving, for speed in attack is the only hope of success against odds.

I went up the stairs like a wraith, close to the wall, moved along the corridor past my own room and went up to the second floor.

There was no sound. I paused in the shadows by the golden door and thought about it for a moment. The next door along the landing was faced with leather and opened to my touch. From the look of it, it had been Hoffer's, and the usual sliding glass doors opened to the terrace on the other side.

I went back into the corridor, flattened myself against the wall and said softly, "Rosa—are you there?"

Her voice was clear and sharp. "Run, Stacey! Run!" There was the sound of a blow and three bullets splintered the door.

I went through Hoffer's room on tip-toe, moved along the terrace and peered in. Rosa was lying on the floor wearing a housecoat. Ciccio was over by the door with his back to me. He was bare-footed, wore pants and a singlet and held a gun in his right hand.

Rosa started to get up as Ciccio opened the door cautiously. I stepped into the room, shot him through the hand as he started to turn. He yelled, the gun jumping out onto the landing and disappearing over the edge.

Rosa had been weeping and her face was badly bruised and her right shoulder—I noticed that as the housecoat slid down to the waist, exposing the upper part of her body, her naked breasts. She covered herself mechanically, an expression of wonder on her face.

"Stacey—Stacey, it is you. They said you were dead."

She flung her arms about my neck and held on tight. I didn't take my eyes off Ciccio for a moment.

"No, I'm not dead," I said, "but Hoffer is—Mafia justice."

"Thank God," she said fiercely. "I wanted to warn you, Stacey, last night after I left your room. I wanted to go back. You were right—I was afraid. Afraid for many reasons, but Hoffer was suspicious. He beat me, then gave me to this—this animal."

Ciccio stepped back and I took her forward through the shadows to where light filtered in from the landing. The bruises on her face were worse than I had realised and something moved like fire in my belly.

"He's had his way with you?"

She didn't attempt to pretend. Her head went back and there was still pride there. "He has my marks on him also."

I turned and at the sight of my face Ciccio went back quickly, still clutching his bloody hand. "Please, signore." He forced a fake man-to-man smile. "This woman is a whore from the back streets of Palermo. Everyone knows what she was before Signore Hoffer took her in."

He smiled again eagerly, his back to the stairs and rage

boiled like lava inside me. "You find it funny? You like a joke? Then laugh this off."

I kicked him in the crotch with all my strength. He screamed as he doubled over and my right knee lifted into his face, sending him back down the stairs. He rolled over twice and crashed to the floor below. He lay there for a moment and then, incredibly, got to his feet and lurched out of sight dangling what looked like a broken arm.

I turned to Rosa. "The day you start feeling ashamed about your past just let me know, I'll let you have a few choice items from my own that should make you feel about as soiled as a Vestal Virgin by comparison. I'm going to leave you now. Burke's waiting for me upstairs in the roof garden."

"No, Stacey, there are two of them. They will kill you."

"I don't think so. On the other hand anything's possible in this life." I took out my wallet and handed it to her. "If it goes wrong, whatever you find in there should help you along the way more than a little. Now get dressed and wait for me downstairs in one of the cars."

I started to turn and she caught me, held me to her yet did not kiss me. She said nothing, but her face was eloquent enough. When I pulled gently away she did not try to stop me.

18

THE DOOR at the top of the stairs stood open, the garden was floodlit again, a place of wonder and delight, sweetly perfumed in the rain.

I paused to one side of the door and considered the situation for a while, then moved along the landing, tried another door and found myself in a study of sorts.

The room was in darkness, the inevitable glass doors that formed the other side standing open. *Which way would he expect me to come, that was the thing*. I stood there in the darkness, drained of all emotion, suddenly tired, caught by some strange fatalism that seemed to say it didn't really matter—nothing mattered. We were on our predestined course, Burke and I. What would be, must be.

I went out through the glass doors in three quick strides and dropped into the green jungle of the garden.

His voice sounded clearly. "Over here, Stacey, I know you're there."

"You and me, Sean?" I called. "No one else?"

"As ever was, Stacey boy." The more Irish he sounded the less I trusted him. "Piet isn't here. He went up to the airstrip with our baggage. We're getting out tonight."

Which was a lie. Had to be because whatever else Hoffer had paid him, there was the bearer bond for fifty thousand dollars in that bank vault in Palermo and as today was Sunday he couldn't possibly have collected it on his return. He wasn't going to leave that.

But trapped by that strange fatalism, I decided to play his game and stepped out through the ferns into a narrow path between vines. He stood at the end on the terrace beyond a wrought-iron table, his hands behind his back.

"What are you holding there, Sean?" I called.

"Nothing, Stacey, don't you believe me?"

"After the mountain—after Cammarata?"

Both hands came into view empty. "I'm sorry about that, but I knew you'd never stand still for killing the girl." He shook his head and there was a kind of admiration in his voice. "But you, Stacey—you. Christ, you are indestructible. I thought you in pieces."

"You're losing your touch, Sean—old age," I said. "If you're interested, you didn't do much of a job on the girl either. She's doing fine. Hoffer's the one who's in trouble. Explaining himself to the Devil about now, I should think."

That got through to him and the slight smile left his face. "You're a bloody swine, Sean," I said. "You always were, only I never saw it before. Nothing on earth could excuse what you did up there on the mountain. You and Hoffer should get on fine when you next meet."

"You wouldn't kill me in cold blood, Stacey, after all we've been through together."

He spread his arms wide. "That's just the way I intend to do it," I told him and Rosa screamed from the doorway behind me.

I swung, dropped on my face, pain tearing at my right shoulder, as Piet Jaeger jumped from the vines no more than seven or eight feet away.

For some odd reason the weapon he clutched in both

hands was a *lupara* which had presumably belonged to one of Hoffer's men; just the thing for assassination at close quarters.

I shot him three times, two bullets catching him in the heart, the third in the throat as he went down, dropping the *lupara*. I turned, the Smith & Wesson ready, and looked into the Browning, rigid in Burke's hand.

"Stuck it in my belt at the rear," he explained. "Who's slipping now?"

"Aren't you going to shed a tear for lover boy?" I asked.

His face went very still. "You bastard, I've wanted you like this for a long time."

"But you needed me, didn't you?" I said. "I only discovered that tonight. You only had them carry me out when I was wounded on the Lagona job because I was essential to you. Without me you were nothing." I laughed harshly. "The great Sean Burke. That's a joke. Every move you ever made, every plan, originated in my head. Without me you were nothing and I thought you were some kind of God. You wouldn't even have got into the Cammarata without me or come within ten miles of Serafino and the girl."

"You poor bloody fool," he said. "You think I needed you for the Cammarata job? You think that's why I brought you out of Egypt instead of leaving you to rot?"

"You've got a better story?"

"Try this." He savoured every word as he spoke. "Hoffer wanted Vito Barbaccia's head, but getting at him was impossible until he hired me and I remembered my old friend Stacey Wyatt in the Hole at Fuad. The problem was getting into the Barbaccia villa—all visitors' cars left outside the gate—but would that apply to Barbaccia's grandson? It was worth a try."

I stared up at him and he laughed out loud, the only time I'd known him to do it. "The two gunmen at the villa that night—they were in the boot of the car. That's how they got in. My idea, Stacey, just like Troy and the wooden horse. Worth bringing you out of Fuad for and it nearly worked."

How true it all was I had no means of knowing, but it seemed unlikely that it would have been the only reason for bringing me out of Fuad. No, he had needed me for Cammarata, however much he tried to deny it to himself now. On the other hand, I had certainly mentioned my grandfather to him in the distant past and a name which meant nothing to him then would have assumed a new importance when first heard from Hoffer.

So, he had used me again. Ironic that in this case I was also the one who had foiled him, but I now understood why he had been so quick to shoot the boy with the *lupara* that night in the garden. The only way of guaranteeing a still tongue.

I got to one knee and he shook his head. "You're wasting your time. I've been counting. One in the garden, one on the stairs, three for Piet. That makes five, which is all you ever carry in that thing, unless you reloaded on the way up."

A game—a monstrous game in which we each played our parts. I shook my head and dropped the Smith & Wesson into my pocket. "No, you're right, it's empty."

"This is it, then, Stacey," he said. "We've come a long way since the Lights of Lisbon."

I picked up the *lupara*. "You know what this is?"

"Sure—Hoffer showed it to me. The Mafia favour them —the traditional way of finishing off a *vendetta*. Not much use beyond six feet. You'd have to get close, Stacey."

"I'll get close," I said, stood up and thumbed back the hammer. "You never amounted to a row of beans without me at your back. Let's see how good you are on your own."

He was right, of course—a sawn-off shotgun spreads

so quickly that I hadn't a hope in hell of really hurting him where he stood, which was a good twenty paces away.

I started to walk, staring death in the face, and Rosa cried out sharply. Somewhere I head a car engine and then another, the slam of doors, voices in the night. Mafia arriving too late.

There was only the rain and Burke standing there at the end of a dark tunnel, his face frozen, every line etched deep, the eyes boring into me so that we were caught togther in our own timeless moment.

And then a strange thing happened. The Browning wavered. He took a step back and then another. I don't know what it was that caused it. Perhaps my relentless approach, my apparent contempt for sudden death, the expression on my face. Whatever it was, he cracked— came apart at the seams.

"Stay away from me! Stay away!"

He took three quick paces back, lurched into the low retaining wall and went over with a desperate cry.

I stood there swaying slightly, then dropped the *lupara*. Rosa was there, holding on to me tightly, crying into my shoulder. I stroked her head absently, then moved to the wall and looked down at him, broken across the steps of the terrace sixty feet below.

When I finally turned, my grandfather was there and Marco, together with three hard-looking gentlemen who clutched machine pistols as if thoroughly accustomed to their use.

"You're too late," I said. "All over."

Barbaccia moved towards me. "You're all right?"

"Me? I'm fine. Just Burke and his boyfriend dead and a couple of Hoffer's thugs chipped up a little. What do you think I'll get? Ten years? Fifteen? Rome doesn't like this sort of thing any more. It's bad for the tourist trade."

He put a hand on my shoulder. "Stacey, listen to me.

All this is nothing. Burke and his friend go so deep under the earth that no one ever finds them. The others, I fix—I fix everything. They know better than to cross Mafia."

"That's good," I said. "That's marvellous, because, to tell you the truth, I've had enough of jails to last me a lifetime and I've got other plans, like taking the first plane to anywhere out of Sicily tomorrow."

He looked completely shocked, reached out an uncertain hand. "Stacey, you don't know what you're saying. You must stay with me."

"Stay with you?" I laughed out loud. "I wouldn't cut you down if you were hanging. I've news for you. I made a very interesting discovery tonight. I found out who murdered my mother—you did."

It was the cruellest thing I could have said, however true, and he wilted, became old before my eyes. I turned and pushed my way past his bully boys, feeling suddenly very, very tired.

I got as far as the door and staggered a little and then there was an arm supporting me. Rosa was there, her face full of pride, and she had stopped crying.

"Let me help you, Stacey."

"Can you cook as well?"

"You've never tasted pasta like it."

"Then you're the girl for me. Only one stipulation. We do things right at the first opportunity. I'm sick of irregular habits."

She started to cry again as we descended the stairs, and I patted her shoulder. "My clothes will still be in my room, I suppose. Pack a bag for me and whatever you need for yourself, and don't forget your passport. I'll see you downstairs. And I'll have my wallet."

She gave it to me and went into her room and I made it down the hall under my own steam. It was raining harder than ever when I went into the garden and moved along the terrace at the front of the villa.

He seemed peaceful enough lying there in the rain, although from the look of him his spine was broken and the back of the skull was crushed.

I thought about a lot of things standing there, but mainly of that first time we'd met at the Lights of Lisbon. If only one could hold moments forever, if only people didn't change, but that was not possible. Life was not like that.

Now I was tired, now all I wanted to do was shelter from the darkness in some corner of warmth and if I was lucky, luckier than most people ever are, Rosa would provide that. Rosa and the piece of paper worth fifty thousand dollars that reposed in the lining of my wallet. And I smiled wryly, remembering Sean solemnly sealing the manilla envelope containing the blank withdrawal form I'd substituted for the real thing that day at the bank.

Poor Sean—poor Sean Burke. I took out the Smith & Wesson, dropped it on his chest and left him there in the rain. A poor exchange, perhaps—for him, but not for me.

FREE
Fawcett Books Listing

There is Romance, Mystery, Suspense, and Adventure waiting for you inside the Fawcett Books Order Form. And it's yours to browse through and use to get all the books you've been wanting . . . but possibly couldn't find in your bookstore.

This easy-to-use order form is divided into categories and contains over 1500 titles by your favorite authors.

So don't delay—take advantage of this special opportunity to increase your reading pleasure.

Just send us your name and address and 35¢ (to help defray postage and handling costs).

FAWCETT BOOKS GROUP
P.O. Box C730, 524 Myrtle Ave., Pratt Station, Brooklyn, N.Y. 11205

Name _____
(please print)

Address _____
City _____ State _____ Zip _____
Do you know someone who enjoys books? Just give us their names and addresses and we'll send them an order form too!

Name _____
Address _____
City _____ State _____ Zip _____

Name _____
Address _____
City _____ State _____ Zip _____